The Price of Happiness 3

A novel by

Casey Carter

Also by Casey Carter

The Price of Happiness 1 and 2

Secrets I Neva Told

D1714486

DEDICATION

No greater love than the love from a mother...

In loving memory

Debra Ann Casey-Carter 12-5-54 wings 1-23-08

Casey Carter

ANYTHING WORTH HAVING IS WORTH FIGHTING FOR...

ACKNOWLEDGMENTS

First and foremost, I thank God for creating such a beautiful mind and heart. I m nothing without Him! The favor I ve been shown throughout my mistakes has left me speechless and thankful. I must say thank you again to my supporters who have rocked with me from the start There s nothing like people who stand behind you and genuinely have love for you throughout anything you seek to do. I love y all. #TEAMCC

B,
I did it. I won t say it was easy without you by my side, but with all you ve shown me, I was able to strap up my boots and get it done. You ve been my support system from DAY 1, giving me that unconditional love people dream of. Even being apart, your presence was felt. Thank you for being that RIDER. My love for you is incomparable and unwavering.

Friends
How many of us have them?
Look at GOD!!!!! 2016 was one of my ruff years. However, because of you I prevailed! So many things are revealed to you that you just can t see if you surround yourself with people who refuse to elevate in life. As you level up in life, you truly do lose people along the way. I heard that somewhere, but never believed it to be true. Some losses were very painful, but others, I just stepped outside myself and looked on. The feeling of watching the bad skin shedding from my body resembled the act of snakes. Despite the wasted years I remain incapable of hate. To those I once loved, I want us all to win!

FLASH BACK

Twenty-One

Nothing Was the Same

LONDON

I HADN'T BEEN OUT THE HOUSE IN DAYS – After the funeral, I was under surveillance damn near all day. I wasn't worried about the cops finding out what I did. I was more worried about Jasper not keeping up his end of the deal of leaving me alone. I was suffering enough! I had murdered my best friend in cold blood, was banned from seeing JU, and pregnant with not a clue what to do. I felt like I wanted to die, but that woulda been too easy. JU was still lying in the hospital, Free was dead, and I was living in a plush apartment, compliments of every lick I committed. I didn't even deserve to live after everything I'd done. That bitch Karma was on my ass every second of every day. I was weak from not sleeping or eating. It seemed like I was sitting, just waiting on whatever came next.

It was six in the evening when the UPS truck pulled up. The carrier had rung the doorbell several times before sticking it in the screen door and leaving. I opened the door and grabbed the envelope to see what it was. Who knew I'd be alone on New Year's Eve? Surely not me! Jasper had me banned from seeing JU. That was all I wanted to do these days.

I opened the envelope, pulling the letter out. It was a certified letter addressed to me from Free. That made me sick to my stomach. It was beneficiary paperwork. Tears fell while I read that everything Free had belonged to me-all money. I balled the paper up and threw it across the room. "Leave me be!" I shouted to no one. Free was still haunting me from the grave.

Although it was dark outside, it was still early. Soon, I'd hear fireworks and gunfire welcoming the New Year. I went to shower and get ready for bed. There was nothing for me to celebrate. I was drying my hair, headed from the bathroom when I noticed my front door wide open. The fuck? My gun was in the car-I forgot to grab it when I came back from the store. Shit... I slowly walked over, glancing outside, but I didn't see anybody. I shut the door, locking it again. I thought about getting my car keys and going to get my gun, but it was cold as hell out there and my hair was still wet. I was about to head upstairs when I saw a shadow from the corner...

"I guess I should've known you would renege on our deal, huh?" I thought about dashing for the door, but I knew I couldn't make it. I wasn't gon' lay down like no weak bitch. If Jasper was here to take my life, he'd better bring it, 'cause my baby needed me. I had no plans on dying no time soon.

Fuck it! I made a dash for the door and was almost off the porch when I was kicked in the back, causing me to fall face first on the ground. The snow on the ground slowed me up some, but I shot back up like my life depended on it. I took another blow to my back. Fuck this shit... Roll over, London! At least SEE what you're up against...

I expected to see Jasper's face, maybe even Chase, but the menace I was staring up at wasn't either... Muthafuckin' Sketch was back from the dead...and ugly as ever! He grabbed my feet, dragging me back to the house. I was kicking and screaming my head off.-so, he stopped pulling and started beating me. He hit me in my head so many times I no longer felt the blows. He started stomping me over and over in my face, my neck... and then my stomach.

"Noooooo!!!" I screamed. I could barely see outta my swollen eyes, but I saw the flash of what I'm sure was a gun.

This was it. That bitch Karma was here and ready to take my life! The image of Free taking his last breath appeared in my mind. JU's blood on my hands was the last vision I had before Sketch sent one shot thru my chest.

"Die, you rat bitch!" was the last thing I heard.

JU

SHIT FELT LIKE A BAD DREAM. They say stay away from the light when you in a dream because it means heaven awaits you, but I wanted to see for myself. I could hear all the conversations going on out there, but I just couldn't open my eyes! My mother cried constantly. Jasper spent more time with me now than I ever remembered. Was I dead? I had a flashback of making love to London on my steps and then it jumps to her holding me on the floor crying. What the fuck was happening to me? I only heard London's voice once and she was apologizing, begging me not to leave. "I'm pregnant, baby...JU baby, come here... I miss you!" I saw London smiling the way she does when she blushing or playing hard to get. She was seductively walking backwards, beckoning with her finger for me to follow her. She was heading to the light! "Come on, baby. You can't stay sleep forever. Wake up, JU. WAKE UP!"

My eyes shot open. All I could see through blurred vision

was who I guess was Jasper sleeping in the corner. The monitor started making weird sounds and Jas shot up rushing over to me. Someone flicked the lights on and several hospital people started checking out all the wires and shit on me. Damn, was I fucked up that bad? Shit made me start wiggling my toes and everything. "Sir, can you hear us? Nod your head yes if you can."

I nodded yes. "Okay, we need you to state your name." "JULIUS KING!" I managed to get out. "Bro..." I called out. Damn, my throat was hurting! "Jasper!" I called out waving for him to come closer. He came. "What's up, Bro? What you need?" he asked. "Where's London?!"

DEANNA

I WAS FLYING THROUGH THE HOUSE looking for my keys. I was in a state of panic trying to control myself. I just got a call from the hospital that Lon was just brought in with no pulse. I damn near lost my mind. I jumped in the car and stabbed out. I had to be doing 100 mph down Woodward, running all the lights, dodging cars and traffic. "What happened, cousin?" I said, beating on my steering wheel. She wasn't leaving me now. I wasn't having that. The tears started to flood my eyes like a storm. I pressed my foot to the accelerator and approached the freeway. I needed my family! I was still doing about a 100 when I saw the ramp. There was a car moving slow, merging as well. I tried hitting the brakes, but the pedal went straight to the floor. What the hell? I was pumping faster and faster trying to stop the car, but it wasn't happening. I turned right to dodge that car and hit the ramp, but I missed, hitting the gate instead and falling over... The last thing I remember is the feeling of flying before everything went black...

MOE

I PLAYED BACK THE SCENE over and over in my mind. I wished I would've just screamed her name or got her attention before she got in the car. If only I had known this would happen, I would have never let her out my reach. I took my time trailing behind her just to see where she was going. The evil and jealous side of me said she bet not be pulling up to see no nigga...so, I followed her, but it seemed more like a race. She was flying through the streets like she knew I was behind her. Was she trying to get away? I went to thinking just that, but the view in front of me erased that thought. She was headed to the freeway and cars were blocking the ramp. She HAD to see them. "Slow down, De!" I said out loud. I panicked and went to blowing my horn. I didn't care if she saw me and knew I was following her at that point. I screamed, "STOP! STOP!" as I laid into the horn, hoping people would move out the way or she would slow down or stop.

My heart dropped as I saw her car fly over the side of the freeway. I slammed on my brakes, hopping out the car so quick my seat belt snatched me back in. I unbuckled it and ran towards the freeway where her car laid upside down in shambles. There was nothing I could do. I knew she was gone. I ran to the car screaming her name. "De, do you hear me? Say something, please!"

I pulled at the twisted metal trying to pry my way inside the car to grab her. I couldn't reach her. I needed to touch her. I needed her. I busted open the back window and I crawled halfway inside. All I could reach was her hair, dangling in midair. Any part of her I could touch was better than nothing. I laid there waiting on the ambulance. I could hear the sirens. I just needed to hold her. I needed to touch her. I laid cramped in the rubble caressing her hair, running my fingers through, for what I felt would be my last time, asking God to please let her live.

The feeling of losing her made me sick. I jumped up quickly trying to catch my breath. Vomit hit my shoes as the EMS arrived. "Sir, please step to the side." I watched as they cut her lifeless body out the wreck. I ran to the stretcher.

"Wake up baby, please!" "Sir, you're gonna have to step..."

"STEP WHAT, NIGGA?! IF YOU TELL ME THAT AGAIN I'M BREAKING YOUR JAW, DOG. THIS MY WIFE YOU ASKING ME TO WALK AWAY FROM! FUCK YOU!" "Sir, I'm sorry. I understand you're upset. Just allow us to get her on the truck and then I'll make sure you can ride along. I see you may need medical attention as well." I looked down and the sleeves of my shirt were full of blood. "Naw, I'm ok. I'm good." The EMS worker insisted I come along. "I'M GOOD!" I screamed. "Just save my wife!" I watched as they pumped up and down on her chest and hooked oxygen to her face. Then the doors closed and off they went.

Blood continued to drip from my hands. Between trying to pry the doors open and busting windows, I really don't know how I caused myself to bleed but I didn't care. My adrenaline was pumping. I could feel no pain of my own. De had taken it all. I ran to my car to follow them to the hospital, praying the entire drive there. I couldn't sit in the back of no ambulance and watch her die. Besides, I saw way too many of my homies leave the street that way and it kinda scared me. I ain't never wanna ride in the back of one unless it was my time, and I'm glad I didn't.

I think praying along the way is what gave me hope, and what gave her another chance. I never asked for God's help before, but I needed it then. As I stood there looking through the window of the ICU revisiting that horrible accident, I couldn't thank God enough my baby was breathing. The doctor walked up from behind and stood there next to me. I gave him a questioning glance out the corner of my eye.

"Hello, you must know the patient." "Yes, that's my wife." "Oh, ok. Well, may I call you, Mr. Black?" "Yeah." "Great. I'll catch you up to speed. Let me start by saying DeAnna is very lucky. I've never seen anyone survive a car accident like hers, and those who have only lived as a vegetable. However, in her case, she only suffered slight hematomas and multiple body inflammations. Our most critical thing to watch is the swelling on her brain, which can cause transient global amnesia. When the swelling dissipates..."

"Hold on, doc. All this vegetables and acute global stuff... I don't know shit you saying. Can you tell me in MY terms what's up? 'Cause I'm not no doctor."

"Oh, I'm sorry, Mr. Black. Basically, she has suffered some minor scrapes and bruising. The most important factor we are watching is the swelling in her brain. As the swelling goes down, she may have confusion or be forgetful, which is what transient global amnesia means. It's only seen in rare cases with strokes and other conditions, which is why she is in

ICU- to rule out any other health problems. Pretty much, she will be ok. We believe her memory is a bit impaired. How long have you guys been married?"

"5 years, why?" He pulled out his notepad and wrote down something. "Umm, hello...why you ask that?" "Well, she seems to believe you were married a week ago."

I frowned in disbelief as the doctor spoke, turning back to stare at De. He patted me on my back. "Nothing to worry about. She will regain her memory as the swelling goes down, and she will continue to wake up for brief moments and then go back to sleep. It's all normal. If you need anything, just let me know. My name is Dr. Patel."

DEANNA

This isn't real. This can't be happening. You have to wake up, you're dreaming. This isn't real. This can't be happening. You have to wake up, you're dreaming. This isn't real. This can't be happening. You have to wake up, you're dreaming. This isn't real. This can't be happening...

No matter how many times I said the words, I refused to believe them. So, I kept running. I was running as fast as I could...so fast I came out of my shoes! I looked around frantically for a place to hide, but there was nothing but darkness and cold. I couldn't make out anything ahead or nearby that would provide safety from the monster chasing me. Ironically, the further I ran away, the more terrified I became. Lightning illuminated my surroundings for only a heartbeat before the darkness swallowed me up again. Rain began to beat my face as I pushed toward the faint light I prayed was not an illusion. The puddles on the ground felt like quicksand under my feet as I continued to try to escape from the unknown.

"Somebody, HELP ME!" I screamed, but I all I heard was the echo of my own voice and what sounded like laughter. I was exhausted and so afraid that I was shaking, but most of all, I was confused. "Why am I running? This isn't real. This can't be happening," I thought. Stopping to catch my breath, I heard heavy footsteps coming from behind, moving at a steady, but quick pace. My heart screamed, "RUN!" and my brain propelled me forward. I turned to run again, only to trip and fall face first, crashing my head against the cement.

I opened my eyes, thankful to escape that horrible dream I was having. "Where am I?" I wondered... I touched my head feeling a wrap or something tied around. It hurt when I touched it. My hands were scraped up and I had a cast on my left leg. Oh, my God. What happened to me?

CHAPTER 1

Finding My Way Back

DEANNA

That was an awful dream I had... I slowly sat up, but the pain that shot through my neck forced me back down. Damn, what the hell did I do? I grabbed the remote and signaled for a nurse to come in. My nurse buddy, Ms. Genie came in with a concerned look on her face.

"Thank God it's you! What am I missing? What's going on?" I asked Genie.

"Slow down De! One thing at a time." she said. "Let's get

your vitals." She seemed nervous, and it was very unlike her to be in such distress. "Genie, what's up? Tell me why I'm here," I pleaded. "You had an accident, babe. It's a miracle you came out with minor scrapes and bruises. For the most part, you'll probably experience some soreness for a couple weeks, but you'll heal.

Do you remember anything before the accident, DeAnna?"

"Umm, not really." I tried, but it was all a blur. "Arghh!!!" I shouted. Genie rushed back over to the bed.

"What's wrong?"

"I keep getting these sharp pains in my neck that hurt like hell."

"I'll get you something for the pain. I'll be right back," she said

I laid back, resting my head on the pillow. I heard the door open again. "Wow, that was quick!" I said, looking up to see it was Maurice. "Hey, you...'

"What's up baby, how you feeling?" he questioned.

"I guess I'm good. My neck is killing me though. What happened to me? Did somebody hit me or something?"

He went on to explain the same thing Genie had stated. His explanation sounded rehearsed as well. I just blew it off. "Is London here, too?" I asked. I knew she would tell me what the hell was going on if nobody else would. He ignored my question.

"You hungry?" Moe asked

"Did you hear me? Where's London?" I asked again, becoming annoyed with everyone's short answers.

Genie came back in the room with an IV pole and medicine. "Well, damn! What did the Doc order?" I asked, raising a brow.

"De, that accident was a bad one. Even if you're not feeling anything right now, it doesn't mean you won't later. We want you comfortable." Genie said.

"I'll be right back," Moe said, making a quick dash for the door. I sat quiet, letting Genie run my pain meds through my IV. I instantly felt groggy. I looked at Genie, about to question her more, but I drifted off to sleep.

MOE

"So, you're just going to allow her to believe this fantasy that you two are in a good place?" Genie asked.

I thought about it for a minute. I really didn't feel I owed this woman no explanation, but I got it. She was looking out for De, but I had that under control.

"At this time, that's what I feel is best. There's no need to get her worked up by having her relive everything we've been through." The doctor said in due time she'd get her memory back. Until then, I had no intentions on fucking up my chances on reclaiming my wife.

I stood at the doorway seeing my girl asleep in a hospital bed. I thought about how she went over the median, almost losing her life. My heart tugged at the thought. I wasn't letting her outta my sight ever again.

My cell buzzed. Seeing it was Bones, I stepped away to take the call.

"What up, fam?"

"You, big dog. What's good? How's the wifey?"

"She resting right now. That was a close call, my nigga. I probably won't be around the next couple days, so hold shit down."

"Oh, fasho! I know she fucked up about her cousin, dog! I knew you'd have to be by her side 24/7!" he said

"Her cousin? What you mean? She had an accident, bro."

"I know dog! That shit gotta be crazy, losing yo cousin and damn near losing yo life!" Bones said.

"Nigga, what the fuck you talking 'bout, losing her cousin? You losing me, dog."

"Damn, my nigga. You ain't heard? Word in the hood is London got busted out in front of her crib, fam."

"Nigga, what? Who the fuck told you that? Hello?"

I lost my fucking signal! I kept trying to call back, but the call kept dropping. I dashed to the nurse's station looking for ole girl. "Aye, I'm looking for Genie. You seen her?" These bitches looking all dumb and shit. My heart was racing…this can't be life!

I tried calling London's phone, but got no answer…WTF! Come on, girl, answer… I saw Genie walking down the hall and rushed over to her. "Aye listen, I know I'm not your favorite person right now, but I need your help." She eyed me as to say, "Yeah, right." "Listen, I just got a phone call that De's favorite cousin was killed tonight." Her eyebrows shot up.

"WHAT?" she said.

"Yes, her cousin London."

"Oh, my God, no!"

She started praying out loud. I didn't want to interrupt and shit, but I needed answers. She walked to the computer and started typing. She then phoned a couple more hospital personnel trying to get more info. Nobody knew shit. I told her to keep her ears open and wrote down my number to give to her. "If you hear anything, call me. I apologize. I don't want De hearing about that, either." She rolled her eyes and walked away. I didn't give a fuck who felt I was wrong, I was doing what was best for me and my wife.

OMAR

I took a taxi back to the house from the hospital. I couldn't wait to see Candace! I was dying to hear the explanation to this here. I made a good decision staying overnight. I felt well-rested and overly alert. I couldn't believe she did that to me. I thought back to the night I came home from work intoxicated and slept with her, shaking my head at the disaster this had become. The sex was good, but she evidently was looking for something more. I started questioning myself on all our interactions, wondering if I played a part in her believing we were becoming something. Outside that one night, I'd say no! Even so, you don't push someone out of a car because of rejection. That couldn't be it… I finally arrived, practically ejecting from the car and running into the house.

"Candace!" I called out. "Candace, are you here?" I walked through, opening all the doors and calling her name repeatedly. I walked in her room to find the bed made and the room spotless. I stood there for a moment. Something was off… I felt it. I opened the closet door and was taken aback. Her clothes were gone. I rushed over to the drawers-same thing. Empty! Yep. Something was certainly wrong. Candace left without notifying me that she quit, nor that she was moving out. "Wow…" I said aloud. I dialed her number, but the call wouldn't go through. This was getting stranger by the second. I phoned the office, but she wasn't there either. Candace was gone, apparently, which was probably for the best, but what happened?

CHAPTER 2

Love Made Me Do It

LEAH

The nightmares were getting worse. I kept waking up in cold sweats, hearing my baby crying for me. It felt so real! I lay in bed night after night holding nothing but my pillow. It wasn't fair we had to be apart, but here I was again, left no choice. I couldn't risk Moe seeing my stomach, so I settled for sending pictures from my phone, fully clothed and holding my belly. He never replied, but I knew he was receiving them because the money in my account never stopped coming. I was thankful for that, because I had to spend a lot of time volunteering in order to get in good graces with the people at the hospital.

Today, I was going house-hunting. I got a list from the bulletin board while I was at work. I thought this plan through from start to finish, even the parts that could possibly go wrong. Several houses, I drove right past. I couldn't believe they had the nerve to even put this mess on the market! I had to have seen over 15 houses. I was almost ready to quit until I came to my last stop. The block looked quiet and the best part about it was it was on a dead-end street. I got out and walked around, scoping out the house on the sides and behind. I stood on a brick and peeked through the window. From what I could see, it looked outdated, but not for long. It would do for now. Once back in the car, I left a message for the realtor to give me a call. I was going to make an offer as soon as possible. Six thousand dollars for a house was a steal. I was so excited to finally be making moves for me and my family. Three-bedroom colonial made just for me, Moe, and the kids.

CANDACE

I knew it wasn't safe to come back here, but shit-I had no choice. Money was low and I didn't have a soul I could count on. I was on my own like I'd been my whole life, but for some reason, it didn't affect me until now. I stared down at the ID picture, then back up at myself in the mirror. "It's just hair, Candace… *it's just hair,"* I repeated. I had been trying to build up the nerve ever since ole boy dropped the new ID off. I love my hair. Not one time did I ever want to cut it. Reluctantly, I reached for the scissors… I closed my eyes, grabbed my ponytail, and before I could lose my nerve, I cut. I didn't stop cutting until my hair resembled Halle Berry's short style. I applied the honey blonde coloring to the hair that remained and waited for results.

I stared at my reflection in the mirror. "Wow…" I said out loud. I looked totally different, but I loved it every bit of it. I thought about all I'd been through and was thankful it didn't show on my face. I still looked youthful and vibrant! This was my last chance to start over and I wasn't going to fuck it up.

Mentally, I was absorbed with everything that transpired in NC with Omar, and for a split second, I felt bad. I tried to make him see the real me and love me back. He was just too stupid and weak to comprehend all that I had to offer him. I couldn't think about that now. Time was ticking, and if I didn't move quickly and efficiently, I'd ruin EVERYTHING.

CHAPTER 3

Strangers

JU

The detectives were riding my ass for a statement. After repeating the same shit over and over, I had nothing more to say. *I was with my girl... A dude came in trying to rob us. I didn't know the nigga...*

Besides, my focus was finding London and getting to the bottom of this shit Jasper was talking about. For some reason, he was insisting Lon set the whole shit up-that couldn't be true. I replayed the scene so many times looking for a clue or something, but came up with nothing. I was gon' find him and make him pay for what he did... I reluctantly rang the bell that sat on the night table. Anytime I tried to get up out the bed, that coughing shit started. I got so short of breath I could barely speak when I went into those episodes. Jasper made it his business to have me brought to his crib with a private nurse and rehab. Shit wasn't so bad. I just felt it was always some hidden agenda with my bro.

Ms. Rosa entered the room in a hurry…

"Baby JU, you ok?" she asked.

She'd been calling me that since I met her. "I need my cell phone. Have you seen it?" She walked to the dresser and grabbed it.

"You need anything else baby?" Rosa asked

"No, I'm good, thank you."

Once she left, I powered my phone up and the notifications started. I had a million messages coming through with people asking if I was okay or get well soon stuff. None from London. Fuck! I wanted some answers and I wanted them now. I dialed her number, and it went straight to voicemail, which was full. I snatched the pillow from behind my head, burying my face in it. How could she not be by my side at a time like this? How could she not be here denying the shit Jas was saying about her? Shit was just baffling to me… I needed to get up and get out! I knew if anyone could find her, it would be me. I sent Jasper a text letting him know I was going home today. I couldn't figure out shit laying here feeling sorry for myself.

"That's it right there," I said to the driver, pointing at the front door of London's apartment. I stared at the porch… The mailbox was overrun with handbills, sales papers hanging from the door. "Go 'head," I said. The driver got out to knock on the door for me. Looking back over to the car, he shook his head no, indicting nobody was home. "Try again," I said. After a while, no one came. He was headed back when a car pulled up, parking next door. The old lady that got out instantly started talking.

"You looking for the young lady that lives there?" she asked.

He looked at me. Is this nigga stupid?! I rolled down the window. "Yes, ma'am, we are looking for her. Have you seen her?"

"Not since that night. New Year's Eve," she said, looking down at something on the ground.

I followed her eyes to an old spot on the ground, clueless.

"It's a shame, she was so young."

Shame? What's a shame? That feeling was in my throat again… I opened the door to get out.

"Sir, you're not well. You shouldn't be getting out of the car."

"Move!" I managed through the coughing and walked only feet away from where the old lady stood. "What's a shame?" She pointed down at the spot on the ground.

"I was asleep when the shots were fired. It frightened me. I almost didn't wanna get up to look out the window, but I did."

My phone started ringing, but I ignored it. The driver heard his ring next and stepped away. "So, did you look to see?" She dropped her head...

"I looked just as the man stepped over her and walked away. I called the police before I went outside, still scared he might return, but I just couldn't leave her out there alone."

For the first time in a long time, tears fell down my face, feeling like ice.

"Are you okay, sweetie? You don't look well."

I took a deep breath and gave my attention to the only person with any answers for me so far. "What else?"

"When I got out there, she was holding her chest, gasping for air. I got down on my knees and placed my hands on top of hers to apply pressure like they say to stop the bleeding, but it was so much blood... I tried, but there was nothing I could do to help her."

I couldn't move from the spot, staring down at what must have been Lon's blood stains on the ground.

"I'm sorry, baby. She was such a pretty girl...so quiet, too. I never seen her bother anyone."

I was barely able to make it back in the car. My girl was dead...and here I was, alive! I flopped my head back on the headrest and allowed myself to openly grieve. I didn't give a fuck if the driver was looking or who saw me. At that moment, I wished I never woke up from that coma. At least I know I would've seen her in my dreams again. I guess when the nigga heard I wasn't dead, he killed her instead…type of hoe shit was that?

DEANNA

I woke up to the voice of Carl Thomas playing from the iHome in our bedroom.

"Good morning, my baby," Moe said, carrying a tray of breakfast.

"Hey, you," I replied, looking at the tray full of fruits and one single red rose lying beside it.

"How you feeling?" he asked.

"Better, just still a little sore." I swung my legs off the bed, planting my feet on the floor. I was over laying in the bed. Before Moe could protest, I was up and walking to the bathroom. I stared at myself in the mirror. "I look a mess," I said out loud. "I have to call Am. I can't go on looking and feeling like shit." Adjusting the temperature to the shower, I stepped in. I stood under the shower head drowning in my thoughts. Everything felt so jumbled in my head. I'd have a thought and then it was gone. I just stood there for awhile enjoying the hot water against my skin. Moe stepped in the shower closing the sliding door behind him. I knew that look in his eyes… sexual hunger.

"I just wanna be near you! When I almost lost you, I broke into a million pieces," Moe said.

He turned, grabbing a face cloth and lathering it up. He looked so worried... "You okay, boo?" I asked.

"I'm good as long as you are, baby girl."

He washed my entire body, paying close attention to the sensitive spots. Everything seemed tender to the touch, and I could tell he was trying his best not to hurt me. I couldn't help but notice he was hard and trying to ignore it. I felt weak and sore, but my hands felt fine. While he was busy rinsing the soap off, I grabbed his swollen rod in my hand and massaged it. Moe braced himself on the shower wall. He bit down on his lip, grunting each time I moved up then down again. Damn, how long had it been? I was thinking hard...

"You gone make me cum, De, don't stop," he said, throwing his hips in rhythm with my hand technique. He leaned in, kissing me rapaciously, moaning in my mouth, still fucking my hand. "Cum for me," I managed to say in between the kisses. Seconds later he did just that... he never stopped kissing me.

"I missed you so much, baby" he said.

"You act like I've been gone forever... One week in the

hospital," I said while rinsing my hand. "I want a rain check later," I told him, pointing down at his manly parts as I stepped out the shower. I wasn't sure why, but I was sexually famished, too. My mind just wouldn't allow me to think about it.

I wasn't cleared to drive yet, so I assumed Moe would drop me off. I continued to get dressed, excited to finally be getting out the house.

CHAPTER 4

All In My Head

MOE

I peeked in on De to make sure she was already in the shower. I rushed to her cell phone to call Amber ass. Strangely, there was a text message on the screen- Jas: missing you Ma.

That shit made my blood boil! I deleted the text message and blocked the number. That must have been the nigga she had dinner with. Part of me wishes I'd never seen that shit, but I had no choice but to look past it.

"Hey Boo, how are youuu?" Amber answered.

"What up, this Moe." She didn't respond right away. I'm sure she was still mad I blocked all visitors while DeAnna was recovering.

"Okay. What?" she said.

"Look, I don't really have time to talk in circles, so I'll make this short. DeAnna suffered some bad trauma to her head, not really remembering a whole lot of shit that's happened. At this time, the doctor thinks its best we leave it alone and let her come around on her own."

"You mean YOU think its best!" Amber chuckled.

"Aye look, that shit wasn't no request! Do her fucking hair and that's it. If anything is said…" The call was disconnected. Oh, this bitch must think I'm playing! I heard the shower turn on, so I placed the phone back on the night stand. DeAnna was humming some song on cloud nine. I could tell she was happy to be getting out of the house, and probably happy to be getting away from me.

JASPER

"You can't shelter him forever!" Rosa said.

I continued eating my breakfast. I knew she was right, but nobody was going to tell me how to protect my brother. He wasn't ready for this cold-ass world, and this incident with that bitch London proved that.

"So, where's the girl?" she asked.

"Who gives a fuck?" I spat, slamming my fork down on

the plate. Rosa glared at me. "Look, excuse my language, but my brother almost died because of some puss…" I caught myself, remembering she was my elder. "As far as I'm concerned, she's lucky I didn't snatch her skull off her neck. Trust me-he will thank me later."

"I'm not sure Mr. King, but I will not get in your family business from here on out!" Rosa said.

She spoke something in her Creole I didn't understand, wiggling her index finger at me. Whatever she said didn't matter. My mind was made up- JU was taking his ass back overseas, ASAP.

"Mr. Ramon is here!" she said.

Chase walked through the foyer greeting Miss Rosa, but she ignored him. I just shook my head. He looked confused. "She pissed at me," I told Chase, "so that means she pissed at you too."

"What you do now?" Chase said, laughing.

"What's the word on ole girl?"

"Shit yet, but believe me, with that twenty stacks on the floor, somebody gone jump to it."

"I meant DeAnna."

"Oh, shit. Amber ain't gave up shit, yet, but I'm on that, too. Something went down, though. I know that much…but I'll have that info later."

OMAR

Thoughts of her retrieved from the depths of my memory, she is golden. Before sleep blankets me she is my last thought. As I dream the night away, her presence so strong that I daydream in the midst of a dream about her. As I wake to the morning sun and drop to my knees, it seems when I thank the Creator for the opportunity to experience another day, I thank Him for creating her. Her not in my presence is sickening… This was worse than any common cold, virus or flu, my cure and vaccination can only be administered through and by her. Preferred to be taken by mouth, but needed immediately like an IV; without her it's like death…the absolute absence of life.

See, her beauty, so profound, not even words manifested, translated and scribed to print can illustrate…. yet she can motivate thoughts into feelings, feelings into wants, wants into desires, desires into necessities to survive. Got damn she is Golden!

She makes me wanna do something, solve a problem, go to confession, join a therapy session, create a moment, anything for her at moment's notice…

I thought about the last time I saw her. Just to be in the same room with her… thoughts of making love to her, but I'd settle just to spoon with her again. *From the flawlessness of her face, to the enticing movement of her hips, she overwhelms me. For God's sake, I pray that would be all mine. But, due in accordance with the Divine, we could be one like melanin and sun in summertime. See it's not the actions with her, but the anticipated journey that excited me. DeAnna is Golden….*

I made up my mind. I was going to have her.

Once my plane landed, my first business was to find Candace. After that, DeAnna was my priority!

CHAPTER 5

Truth Be Told

CANDACE

"Why didn't you tell me the brakes you had my brother clip was that lady's that came up to the college?" Samantha questioned.

"Why you so worried about it? You act like you knew the bitch or something."

"I was suspended from work today Candace! They are questioning those documents I made you and what if this other shit we did gets out?" Samantha said.

"WE? I didn't do a got damn thing," I said, looking her square in the face and contemplating my next move.

"What?" she said, pacing back and forth on the worn-down carpet. "So, this is on me and me alone, huh? That's what you saying, Candace?"

"What I'm saying is I'm denying anything that could land me behind bars and I'd advise you to do the same." She stood there silently. I glared right back at her ass.

"If that's how you wanna play it after everything I've helped you with, cool with me! I'll be sure to save my own ass and *YOU* do the same," Samantha said, leaving and slamming the door behind her.

Once she left, I plopped down on the bed. The nerve of this bitch to think that I would help save her ass if it came down to it. Don't get me wrong- she has helped me out a lot, but I barely could save my damn self. All caught up in my thoughts, I picked up a bottle of vodka that was on the table and threw it at the wall. "Fuuuuuucccck!" I yelled out. I was ready to be on an island somewhere relaxing, not ducking & dodging bullets.

DEANNA

"Why are you acting weird?" I asked.

Laughing, "What do you mean De?" she asked.

"I've just missed you, friend, that's all."

She washed my hair and rambled on about the gossip at the shop. I closed my eyes and relaxed. Once in her chair, I noticed stares and whispers.

"So, what's up, Miss Thing? You feeling better?" Amber asked.

"Yeah, I'm better. Just some soreness and these horrible ass headaches…thanks for asking boo. Moe has been very compassionate. You should see him girl…"

"Yeah, I bet!" Am mumbled.

That's the second time I heard her mumble something like that.

"What's up with you?" I asked.

"Nothing girl, I was just saying. You know how Moe is. I'm sure he was terrified of almost losing you after that accident. That's all I meant sweetie, relax," she said.

I'll tell you this: I was becoming irritated with everybody acting strange and shit.

*****

AMBER

This shit wasn't right at all. The nerve of that sick bastard forcing me to lie to my best friend, let alone threaten me if I told her anything… Little does he know I basically saved his got damn life, 'cause had I told Chase, it would have been major problems. She looks so lost and confused… I was hoping and praying she got her memory back. Mr. Maurice thinks he's gonna trick her into thinking they were happy-go-lucky, but this was definitely gonna blow up in his face. I was wondering what he did with that lunatic of a girlfriend he was cheating on my girl with. She couldn't be far. Regardless, I wasn't no gangsta, but until my girl was back to herself, it was up to me to protect her.

When I got home, Chase was there sitting on the sofa. Just like that, my bad day was a thing of the past. I was so excited. "Hey, you!" I squealed, plopping down on his lap.

"What's up Shorty," Chase said, kissing my forehead.

Him finally using his key made me so happy. I could hardly contain myself. "How long you been here? You hungry?" I asked.

"Hell yeah! What you got in there?"

"Little bit of everything," I replied, not wanting to give away the fact that I purchased all his favorites when I went to the market.

"Whatever you whip up is fine."

I hopped off his lap and pranced into the kitchen to get my boo together.

I decided on some pepper steak and rice. Chase loved steak, plus it was something quick and easy. The faster I finished the sooner I would be back in his arms.

"So what you been up to? Hanging with the weirdo?" he asked.

I laughed, "She's not weird, she just has to know you."

"Well good thing she knows me now, then."

I fell quiet. Looking back over his shoulder he asked, "What's wrong Ma?"

Sadness suddenly fell over me again. "Actually, she doesn't know you, again." He laughed.

"No, like seriously," I said, peeved.

"What are you talking 'bout Am? We talking about yo girl De, right?"

"Yeah." Softly, I begin to explain how she had an accident a couple days ago, and lost pretty much a lot of her memory of current events.

"So, does she remember you?"

"Of course, she does. Basically, anything that has happened in the last year is a blur for her." I waited for him to reply. "I've been trying to get her out of the house, but it's so complicated now." I couldn't explain the situation about Moe for fear he'd tell his boy. If De hadn't told him her business, it wasn't my job to do it. Besides, who knows if she would ever see him again after all this?

"So, where she at?" Chase asked.

"She's home." This was the most Chase had asked for as long as I'd known him. I decided I'd change the subject to prevent slipping into a forbidden conversation about my girl.

LEAH

"You have a phone call at the desk," Veronica the nurse said. I didn't like her too much. She was always making side jokes, eyeing me and shit. I couldn't stand nosy ass women who couldn't mind their business. Ever since that day, I smacked her hand down when she reached to touch my stomach. Now she walks around staring or whispering about me to her little entourage. I couldn't care less. I was here for one reason only…my son! This was the call I was waiting for. I wrote down all the details, excited about all my plans coming together. I couldn't wait to get off and get the ball rolling. I continued my day humming through the halls like I just hit the jackpot, counting down the hours 'til it was time to get off.

"Congratulations, Ms. Thomas," the realtor said, shaking my hand.

I walked out with my keys to my new home in hand, ready for a new start. Everything was coming along as planned like I knew it would. All I had left to do was get Moe on board. I headed home to complete more packing. It was time move to the next task. God was really blessing me.

CHAPTER 6

A Life Worth Living

LONDON

Prayer:

Psalm 23:4

Yea, though I walk through the valley of the shadow of death, I will fear no evil: for thou art with me; thy rod and thy staff they comfort me...

Grandma said there'd be days like this. Everything was hurting like crazy! I just kept my eyes closed so they'd think I was sleep and allow me to suffer alone. I didn't have shit to say no way. My life was fucked up! I knew sooner than later

I'd have to right my wrongs, but I guess I was moving too slow. My right hand was cuffed to the hospital bed, my left hand cuffing my belly. My son…the purest part of me. He was made from love. I was at my best when he was planted inside me, a gift I wasn't even sure I deserved. All that I have loved…I lost! Free… JU… was God planning on making me suffer more? I didn't give a fuck about anything that could happen to me at this point. I deserved it all. But Saint, my sweet baby boy, he was innocent. I prayed he was everything of JU and none of me.

I heard footsteps, then the sound of the door opening.

"She's stable, so whatever you all need to do, go ahead."

I felt someone touch my left hand that lay firmly on my belly. My eyes shot open. "Don't fucking touch my stomach!" One nurse and two cops were standing at the foot of the bed.

"London Green…

You have the right to remain silent. Anything you say can and will be used against you in a court of law."

I didn't say a word! With Sketch still out there, jail might have been the safest place for me. I was wheeled off and shoved into the back of a police car. I rode silent. Jasper probably filled JU in on everything by now. Tears rolled down my cheeks remembering every last memory of JU and me. I'd never loved a man or cared for one the way I did JU. If I was sure about anything, I knew he'd never forgive me... I'd bet my life on that.

CHAPTER 7

The Blame Game

JASPER

I walked out of the building free as a bird! No more parole, no more reporting or having muthafuckas all in my business. Chase hit me up saying he wanted me to meet him to chop it up. Shit sounds important. Today was a good day, so hopefully there was no bad news he wanted to tell me. I turned the radio up and listened to J.Cole's *Neighbors*, bobbing my head, cruising through my old stomping grounds, admiring how there weren't many abandoned houses left and the streets were clean. Because of me, fiends knew better than to stand on corners seeking drugs if schools or playgrounds were near. It's not what you do, it's how you do it. Although

I supplied these streets, it wasn't my hope to ruin it for the kids, making it unsafe to play outside. Words travel fast and in no time, only paging systems were being used for purchasing and after hours smoke shops where fiends could come and do they thang. Whatever made money under the radar, I was with the shit.

My phone buzzing grabbed my attention. I listened as ole girl gave me the rundown on little Miss London. Just like I thought, she hit many licks on niggas. "Never trust a bitch with funny eyes…" I thought to myself. State had her on all types of shit, trying to sit her ass down for a minute. She was lucky to be alive and in custody. If it wasn't for her, my brother wouldn't be all fucked up.

MOE

"Have you ever been cheated on?" Leah said through the door.

"Man, fuck all that. Open the fucking door, Leah, and stop bullshittin'". My patience was thin as hell. I just wanted to say what I had to say and get the fuck on.

"I see you changed the locks. That's cool. Just let me in so I can talk to you for a minute."

"Nah, I'm good! Not taking any chances on you trying to

hurt me or my baby. Go away and leave us alone," she said.

I stood there for a second. Why did I come over here? I didn't owe this bitch no explanation! My father ain't teach me shit. My mother stood in for everything. I didn't wanna be a failure to my seed just because I considered the mother a mistake, but I didn't want nothing from this woman. She served her purpose and I was done.

"You know what? You just made it easier for a nigga. Lose my number and don't contact me again. I don't want nothing to do with you or that baby you carrying, so do whatever the fuck you want. I'm out…"

I burned rubber away from her shit, swearing never to return.

Whether anybody believed me or not, I felt guilty. All my life I've been a ladies' man, viewing hoes as toys. Like a selection cars or a variety of watches, clothes, or shoes, I just liked hearing niggas compliment my taste in everything, including bitches. I cheated, but it ain't have shit to do with how I felt about my wife. I loved her during, after, and still. It's just my love for praise and respect through my hood made me feel more like a man than my woman could. The streets when you winning gon' always treat you like that nigga! Like a King, basically, where the woman he loves might not always give him that treatment due to familiarity. A man needs everyone to recognize and compliment his accomplishments. De loves me for me! It's so easy to take her for granted 'cause she's always at home waiting. Being a go-getter like myself, I love the chase, the challenge. I always felt it was nothing I couldn't have, or shouldn't have. That's what made me a hustler. I always tried to prove people wrong, while hurting the one that believed in me no matter what. I fucked up!!! Got this bitch pregnant AGAIN and ain't shit I can do about it. Leah reinstalled that feeling De gave me when we met. It was easy to get confused, thinking the grass was greener, but that's a muthafuckin' lie. Most men don't think past Go. We just some opportunists.

CHAPTER 8

Tears On My Pillow

LEAH

"Mommy mommy… who are you talking to?" Jonathan asked.

I was sitting in the corner of my room trying to escape my thoughts,but I couldn't. I don't even know how long I was sitting there.

His voice wasn't the only one I heard. Stuck in a daze, I tried to focus like I was taught in therapy, but it wasn't working. I closed my eyes for a minute to calm my nerves. When I opened them, my mother was standing there laughing.

"You thought you could live happily ever after, huh, silly?" she said,

*hysterically laughing and pointing at me. "There's no happiness for you,
sweetie. Your life will end up just like mine."*

"Shut the hell up! You don't know anything!" I shouted."
I'm not weak like you. I won't take my own life like a
coward!" The laughing didn't stop. I snatched the lamp off
the dresser and launched it at her face. It slammed against the
wall, making a crashing sound as scattered glass flew
everywhere. Jonathan's loud wails finally grabbed my
attention. He was covering his face with his hands. I rushed
to him, praying I didn't hurt him. Removing his hands from
his face, he snatched away and ran.

"Leave me alone!" he cried.

Running behind and grabbing him again, he started
kicking and screaming, shouting I wasn't his mother and
saying he hated me. I knew he was scared and didn't mean it,
but it didn't stop my heart from hurting. I know I need to go
get meds, but that wasn't an option now. All that does is
make me second-guess my decisions, and I didn't have time
to go there.

LONDON

*"Dirty Red...broken, scared and alone. Look at you, girl, laying
there hopeless! You murk me and then bitch up???" Free laughed
uncontrollably. I knew I was dreaming.... Free was dead... how was he*

still fucking with me from the dirt?

"What you gone do Red? Everybody want a piece of that pretty ass!" he said.

"You're dead!!! Get the fuck outta my head!" I shouted.

"Long as you still breathing, I'm never dead... I told you a long time ago when we made that pact it would always be us, Red. Remember your sixteenth birthday?"

I sat straight up in my bunk in a cold sweat from another nightmare. How could I forget? Somewhere stuck in between darkness and light, my nightmare turned into a dream taking me back to age 16. Free planned a day for me from start to finish. We caught the bus to Fairlane Mall for dinner and a movie. Inside the mall, he pulled out a sock and gave it to me.

"I've been saving 50 bucks every month since your last birthday. Spend it however you want!"

I did just that, but I bought matching dog tags for Free and me.

I just couldn't believe things ending up the way they had.

Every day, I wrote JU a letter. I just never mailed it out. I probably was the last person he wanted to hear from, anyway. I'm almost sure his evil ass brother told him all types of shit about me. I couldn't worry about shit I couldn't fix. Besides, my main concern was Saint, now. Hopefully, when the time comes, I'll be able to redeem myself and he'll love me again.

I had no appetite! I couldn't eat nothing. I could barely

hold water down. I always heard when women get pregnant they gain weight, but I had lost everything. They had me on some high-risk stuff because of them saying something about the baby being small. I kept having these fainting spells, waking up on the floor of my cell with Callie standing over me yelling for help.

Callie and I from jump hit it off. She seemed a lot like me, but very quiet. She became my outlet in this place. I basically told her everything from start to finish. When I was done, she laughed hysterically for 5 whole minutes. I wanted to beat her ass.

"Yeah, your life was fucked up," she said.

The way she said it made me laugh, too, though. She didn't blame me for Free, and that made me feel a little better. But JU... I couldn't stop the tears. I wanted his forgiveness.

I had court in a couple weeks for sentencing. At the most, I was looking at 2- 15years for conspiracy. What's fucked is this one, I didn't have any parts in. I didn't even know the muthafuckas in the court pointing me out. I didn't complain at the time. I needed some safety to protect my baby and that's exactly what I told my lawyer.

The only person I wrote was De, and she never responded. That wasn't like her. I tried calling her phone and everything, but the mailbox stayed full. I gave the number to my attorney to call, hoping she'd get through. I needed to hear from somebody on the outside to know my people were okay.

CHAPTER 9

Half Crazy

MOE

Last night

    This shit I couldn't put in words. After almost a year of not being inside her, I didn't know what to do. I wanted to abuse it, use my dick as a weapon to rip through all the walls then lick her wounds away...

    "Hurry, I can't wait any longer," she said.

    Without one word, I slid inside her, barely able to hold my nut and she opened right up for me. I cried! Cried for all the pain I caused her while remembering all the disappointment I saw in her eyes. I nearly choked on my own betrayal each time I pushed deeper inside her. I gave away parts of me that I vowed only to share with my wife. Recalling the moments, it was Leah under me, calling my name, confessing her love for me. I buried my face in her neck, too embarrassed to look into her eyes. Damn, how I missed her moans and the way she held onto me firmly, calling my name. I was lost inside her, wishing I'd never broken our promises, regretting ever laying eyes on Leah. I had to right my wrongs. I had to tell Leah it's over and mean it.

DEANNA

Finally! I was so excited to finally hang out with my girl. Since the accident, everyone has been hovering over me, making a big deal out of nothing. I rushed to the closet deciding on what to wear. "Damn!" I said out loud. What was I gonna tell Moe? Out of everybody, he's been the most protective. Last night, we went back and forth about me getting another car. He insists on telling me I'm not ready to be back behind the wheel, but I feel fine. Granted, after seeing my car on the pictures, it's a wonder how I made it out of that alive. Had to be the grace of God over me!

I headed down the steps calling out for Moe, who didn't answer. I didn't see him, either. I was just about to call his cell when I heard his voice coming from our attached garage. "Oh, no wonder he couldn't hear me. He must be on a call," I thought. Once I got closer to the door, I heard the voice of a woman. I stood there by the back door, barely cracking it open.

"I tried playing nice, yesterday, but you was on that tuff shit. Now you wanna come all humble and act like shit all good. I'm happy you played the shit like that. I'm done with that shit like I told you yesterday. She doesn't remember none of that bullshit you started," Moe said harshly.

"Bitch, I got my life back; now get the fuck on and don't ever come back! You knew who and what I wanted from the jump," he said, shoving her away.

I looked on, dumbfounded by what I'd just seen. I eyed the woman closely, her face twisted in an upward frown, glaring at Moe with evil-looking eyes. Before she turned and walked away, I caught a glimpse of her round belly.

"This is the last time you'll hurt me!" she said, looking over her shoulder at Moe one last time.

I quickly pushed the door closed and headed back upstairs before Moe could even see I was there. I heard him slam the door. I wasn't exactly sure what went down, but I was surely gonna find out. For now, I decided to keep it to myself, knowing that if I brought it up now there was no way I'd get out this house tonight.

When Moe entered the room, I was laying my outfit across the bed.

"Did I forget a date or something?" he said scratching his head, looking confused.

"Nope! I'm going out with Amber," I said. Before he could protest, I asked again, "Have you heard from London?" As I suspected, he avoided my eyes like he does every time I mention London's name.

Moe walked into the bathroom. "You know how your cousin is De. She disappears all the time for long periods. That's nothing new."

"Yeah, but not coming to the hospital after the accident was totally unlike her; don't you agree? Did you even call and tell her what happened?"

"Of course I did!" he answered.

Although I acted as though I didn't notice, I saw him ignoring his cell phone that kept lighting up. "Well, tomorrow we need to go by her house, unless you want Am to take me."

"Nah," he responded sounding irritated.

"Cool, we'll go tomorrow then."

I continued getting myself together while Moe sat still watching me. Mentally, I could tell he was preoccupied with whatever that was that just went down in the garage with that chick. Every day felt crazier to me, almost like I got disconnected somewhere. Moe acting suspicious, London nowhere to be found and Amber acting funny too... All this had me feeling crazier by the second. All of it was just too much. I needed a break.

"Getting away from Moe has been hard as hell," I told Amber. She continued to drive as I rambled on and on about how good things had been between Moe and me. "I'm not sure what changed but he's totally different," I said. I got tired of the awkward silence... "What's wrong with you?"

"Nothing. Why you ask that?" Am asked.

"I mean, I've been going on and on about my life and you haven't said one word."

"To be honest, I don't want to talk about Moe! Lately that's all we talk about," she stated with her eyes fixed on the road.

I thought about what she said, and maybe I have been a little selfish these days. At that moment, I decided I'd refrain from saying too much to anyone. I watched the snow fall through the passenger window. "So, what's up with you lately?" I asked, trying not to sound too dry.

"Well, Chase and I are really good." she said.

"Chase who? Is he new, and how long do you plan on keeping this one?" I joked. She took her eyes off the road for a second...

"I've been dating him for a minute now. You've met him, but he's fairly quiet. You probably won't remember him."

I laughed. "Girl, what? I don't forget nothing," I said, "especially your flings." She didn't laugh, but she did look at me strangely as if to say, "yeah right." I felt bad.

"Am, lighten up! Damn, I was kidding."

"You're fine, friend," she said, pulling into the lot of Southern Fires restaurant.

"You okay? How's your head? No headaches or anything, right?"

"Girl…chill out! You're acting like Maurice. I'm fine. If I feel like anything, I'll tell you."

We walked in, gave our RSVP and headed to be seated. I didn't remember the inside looking this good. The updates were nice as hell.

****

JASPER

"Chances make champions," that's what I was told. How would I know if I didn't at least try to see if she remembered me? I saw Chase and Amber talking by the bar so I used the opportunity to push up on DeAnna. I waited for the right song to approach her. Women love that shit when the lyrics be on point at the perfect time. I had already sent the waitress to request it so I was waiting for the perfect time. I wanted to jog her memory back to the day we were riding in my convertible '64 Impala with her hair blowing in the wind. She looked bored sitting in the corner. I was about to say fuck it when I heard the sound of Ro James, *Permission*.

Oh, oh, oh
With your permission
I just wanna spend a little time with you, ooh
With your permission
Tonight I wanna be a little me on you, oh yeah
With your permission
I wanna spend the night sleeping on you
You know what I'm talking about baby, yeah
Now it's time for you to show me what it's hitting for
Sip a little jack, maybe blow a little draw
Love you from behind but I hate to see you go
Oh hoo
Come on give me that green light…..

"What kind of perfume is that you're wearing?" I ask, leaning in to smell the nape of her neck. She jumped, scooting over out from under me.

"*Illicit Flower* by Jimmy Choo." she replied.

"It smells damn good on you, Ma." She thanked me, shifting in her seat nervously. I watched her sing along with the music looking fine as hell. Yeah, I don't know about this little "hold the secret" shit, especially after my encounter with that nigga. Who was he to her? Not that I gave a fuck, though! Shidd, as much as I was in her bed, he couldn't be too much of nothing. I was fresh off parole not looking for any trouble. But if trouble happened to come, I had no problems getting rid of the shit.

"You like this song, huh?" I asked, observing her feeling the lyrics.

"I do," she said.

"Yeah, it had a nice little beat to it. I listen to it when I'm riding in my old school." I searched her eyes when she looked up at me thinking she was remembering...then she said "That's nice," and turned her head.

Oh well... I knew it was only a matter of time before all her memories came back. I couldn't wait.

LEAH

What the fuck was she doing there? I drove like a bat outta hell away from that house. The fact that he just disrespected me like that had me ready to turn this car around and run this bitch dead smack into the front door. It wasn't gonna fly this time. I saw that bitch staring from the door. "Moe wants to play dumb and act like he doesn't have to acknowledge me," I said, rubbing the concealed pillow strapped to my body. He had me fucked up.

CHAPTER 10

Far Away

OMAR

I placed the flowers on the ground in front of my mother's headstone, deeply sighing. It felt like much time had passed since the last time I'd been here. They finally placed my father's headstone next to hers, and just like that, they were back together again. I couldn't help but think about my life with DeAnna. With her, I was able to live again and be myself. I still remember the glow my father had on his face when she and I first met. It was almost like he passed away peacefully knowing I'd found a love to share the rest of my life with. I wasn't sure exactly what the future held. I just had hopes that she was in it. I wanted to grow old with DeAnna and, God-willing, walk into Heaven's gates together in the end.

I checked into the hotel, mentally exhausted with everything that's happened in the past year. I wanted nothing more than to be able to live stress free without all the unnecessary BS life kept throwing my way. There *had* to be an ending to the madness. This just couldn't be the plan God had mapped out for me.

JU

I'm not sure what hurt worse, the fact that she was gone, or the fact that I wasn't there to protect her. I found myself stuck in a funk. I didn't wanna be around nobody. Shit, no one understood what I was going through without my girl. I kept having dreams about her. The shit felt so real.

"JU baby …come here, I miss you!" I had that same dream

every night, damn near. I couldn't accept she was gone, not now, not ever.

My mother had mostly been here since the shooting, refusing to go home until I was completely healed. There was no use in trying to convince her to leave because she wasn't having it.

"You hungry, Julius?" she asked from the kitchen.

"Nah, Ma, but come here for a minute."

"What's wrong baby?"

"If I ask you something, you'll tell me the truth, right?" She paused for a minute, then nodded.

"Of course I will, JU. What's wrong?"

I reached for her hand and pulled her down on the couch to sit next to me. "I need to know what happened at the hospital. Not the watered-down version, I mean the real thing." She looked away.

"You know your brother only wants the best for you, right?" she asked.

When I didn't respond, she kept going.

"When I got the call, I can't begin to describe to you what I felt. I got there as soon as I could, baby! Jasper filled me in on what he heard. ...I just couldn't believe it," she said with sadness in her eyes.

"What did he say?"

"Someone told him that London set you up and the guy

she worked with was the one who did that to you."

She continued…

"When I met her, she didn't look as if she was capable of that type of deception… but then again, looks deceive us all the time. You know how your brother is with acting out before looking into things when it comes to us, so after I checked on you, it was my intention to go and ask her about those rumors, but she was gone."

I sat there dazed by what my mother just told me. Replaying everything, all encounters, every conversation, I just couldn't see it. I thought back on that night of the shooting.

"This a Stick- up, muthafuckas," he sarcastically said.

"Look dog, let my girl go and we can settle wateva nigga."

He looked me dead in my face and said, "It's settled, then, Braveheart!"

He fired two shots into my chest…….

I fell back against the wall, sliding down to the floor.

"Run, baby," I said in between gasping for air…

"Be careful who you fall for, Red. You just might have to fall with them… Death before dishonor, bitch!!!!!!!!!!"

"SOMEBODY HELP US!" she screamed…

"JU please please please don't leave me…I need you!!!" London screamed….

"Death before dishonor…" I repeated the words over and

over trying to figure out with the fuck I missed…

"Honestly Ma, what you think?"

"It's not what I think, baby, it's what you feel! Go with your gut. But I will say in the moments I did have a chance to see London, she appeared shattered. At your bedside, sorrow was written across her face. I can't say whether or not she's capable of this type of thing, but if she is, she's a good actor because I believed she truly cared for you," she said, getting up from the couch to answer her phone.

If she wasn't guilty like Jasper thinks, why would she run away like that? There were questions only she could answer, and now that she's gone, I'll never know if this was all some bullshit.

CHAPTER 11

Wait For Me

LONDON

"You sleep?" I whispered out to Callie.

"Nah! What's up?" she said.

"I didn't know what to say or how to say it. Just want to say thank you for helping me get my head on straight in here. You don't know me from a can of paint, yet you still thought enough of me to make sure I had whatever I needed. I owe you big time."

"You don't owe me boo! Where I'm from we look out for

our own, period. You just going through a rough patch, but that shit will pass." Callie said.

I knew she was right, but I couldn't see past the immediate turmoil. Callie going home tomorrow, and that means I'm back on my own once again.

"So, you gone tell him or what? You know if you allow others to be your voice, you sure to be fucked on him forgiving you."

Callie was right, but what would I say? "I was gone set you up *BUT…*" Nah, I knew JU and nothing I could say was going to make it better. I fucked up! I just hoped that when the time came, he would let me explain. That was all I could ask for, and more than I deserved. If he didn't forgive me, then I just had to understand.

CHAPTER 12

The Plug

MOE

"Fuck these niggas at?" I thought in my head, waiting for Chase to pull up with the new connect. The numbers sound so good, I can't miss out. Plus, I know if Chase fuck with him, I can fuck with him. Another 30 minutes go by… Now, this shit strange… he ain't replying to my text or called for anything. A black Suburban pulled up. I set my Glock on my lap, prepared to blow a nigga if I had to. I see Chase hop out. I relaxed knowing everything good. "… ain't this a bitch," I thought. I see the hoe ass nigga that was eating with DeAnna that night at the restaurant. I hopped out ready to blow this nigga! I slowed my stride, deciding I wasn't gone act up unless I had to. This clown ass nigga had the nerve to start smiling. My blood was boiling at this point.

Chase shook my hand...

"This my mans I was telling you about…"

Nigga had the nerve to reach his hand out. I looked at it and spit on the ground. He laughed, "That's how you do the hand that's been feeding you?"

"Feed me? Ain't nobody feeding me, nigga. Imma eat even if I gotta take the next nigga plate."

I had a voice in the back of my head saying, "Kill this nigga." It took everything in me not to up my shit. Chase stepped in front me.

"Man, slow down with all that! The fuck going on?" he asked, looking back and forth.

"We here for business," Chase said.

"Ain't no business to discuss with that nigga. His shit ain't getting moved through none of my spots." The nigga laughed. "Something funny?" I spat.

"Yeah, YOU, little homie. I'm going to pretend this little talk we had didn't happen on the strength you've been bringing me income for quite some time. So, either way I win. Ain't shit gon' change; it's always a hungry nigga ready for the opportunity. Anything that gets moved on these streets come by me first," he said.

"I don't give a fuck! I ain't fucking with you and neither is my runners." I turned to leave.

"Oh yeah- stay away from DeAnna."

He laughed, "Yeah... that's mine, too," before climbing in the truck.

Yeah, this nigga had me fucked up fasho. He'd find out how much sooner or later.

CHAPTER 13

Mind Games

JU

Sadness turned into depression; depression turned into resentment. I was driving myself crazy wondering which stone to turn to find the truth. I slipped my hand behind the mailbox. The key was in the same place it always was. I unlocked the front door and went inside, closing it behind me. The placed smelled stale and empty, even though all of her things were still neatly in place. Feeling like I was ready to pass the fuck out, I kept going, anyway. I walked around her apartment searching for something, shit, ANYTHING that would ease what was left of my mind. I tried, but I couldn't let go!

A cup of juice with mold floating in the glass was sitting on the dining room table. That must have been what she was doing before whatever went down. I walked over to it and stood there…

Next to it was an envelope, but no papers were inside. Curiosity had me. I looked around for a second, but didn't see any papers laying around. I was headed upstairs when over by the couch, I saw a balled-up piece of paper. I picked it up, straightened it and read…

Beneficiary Designation:

In the event of my death, any balance remaining in the participant's IDA shall be

distributed within 30 days of the date of participant's death to the assigned beneficiary, London Green.

The fuck? I was confused. Who the fuck was Jason? And why was she upset about him leaving her all this money? $100,000…why would she be mad about that? Everything about this shit was strange…was that why she was murdered? Did someone know she had this bread?

I was working myself up off some shit I would never know. I went upstairs, against my better judgment, but I just had to. Looking around her room picturing all of the things she used to do, I sat on her bed remembering the last time I made love to her…

I kissed her forehead first before pulling her dress over her head.

"I'm kindly asking for it Ma..."I said ,sitting down on a step and forcing her to straddle me.

With a firmer hold around her waist, I eased myself inside her. It had only been about a week since we'd fucked...

"Damn you tight baby. Relax I got you! You gon' make me ask again?"

I forced it in, causing her to cry out my name. "What do you want?" I asked, barely able to speak between thrusts and our moans.

"Arghh ,"I grunted. " I want you... I want all of you...not just this pussy. I want youuu.

Don't be scared London." I was open. "You thief...you stole it..."she said! I had her heart.

CANDACE

Sitting here pondering, waiting for the time to come for this flight... I can't for the life of me keep calm to get some rest. This sleazy motel wasn't my idea of a getaway. My mind kept racing. I tossed and turned in the bed, then paced the floor, thinking of my past and planning for my future... scanning channels to see if any more of my bad behavior had surfaced on the news. My tablet beeped. I opened it to check my email. It was Spirit Airlines. Those bitches kill me. The fucking flight was delayed. Dammit!!!!! I damn near gave myself a headache, trying to figure out what to do. See, that's why I hate flying with them… I should have flown Southwest. I grabbed my purse, rushing out the door headed to the airport in hopes of getting my money back from Spirit and finding another airline to fly with. I called an Uber, and was waiting in the lobby for the car to pull up. A text came in to my phone: "A black Cadillac CTS should be picking you up in 2 minutes."

Sure enough, they actually pulled up quicker than I thought. As I proceeded to walk out the revolving doors, the driver's door swung open and a man jumped out. He stood with his back to me, dusting off his jeans and fixing his shirt. Instantly, another car just like it pulled up. I froze in my step. A quick glance at the guy and my heart jumped out my chest. I did a u- turn and took off running into the lobby bathroom. I ran so fast my foot slipped out my heels. The ankle strap was still fastened tightly around my ankle as I dragged the shoe behind me, running across the floor. I locked the door and sat on the bathroom floor. Urine began to wet my underwear…I saw someone who sent chills down my spine. Jasper!! Damn… did he see me? Was I seeing things?

I thought about peeking out the door but I was too scared, thinking the moment I opened the door, I'd be staring into the barrel of a gun. I sat there thinking of my next move. A knock at the door startled me. I waited for whoever it was to walk away. I strained my ear trying to hear the voices at the front desk. All I could hear was a woman asking about someone calling for an Uber. I cracked the door open to see the receptionist on the phone. She caught me peeking out. "Hey, ma'am, did u call for an Uber?" I whispered, "Yes, but tell them that's ok."

When she hung up, I made sure the coast was clear before dashing to the elevators. I rested my head on the elevator walls as it stopped at every damn floor before it reached mine. I watched out the window of the elevator as the two Cadillacs pulled off. Did he have a room here? Was he following me? Was it a coincidence? Or had karma finally caught up with me?

CHAPTER 14

Consequences

JASPER

There was nothing stopping me from firing a shot and peeling her shit. She looked dead smack in my face, probably thinking she saw a ghost. "Calm down, bitch: it's not your time," I say, as if she could hear inside the car. Nothing like having people on deck to gather up some info when you're in need... It was only a matter of time before revenge would be mine. I pulled up on JU so I could check up on him. "Little bro what's good?" I asked, walking in on him watching the basketball game.

"Shit." he replied.

"You getting your strength up so you can get back out there on the court?"

"Maybe, maybe not!" he said, sarcastically.

I know this nigga was going through something, but I was getting sick of his snappy ass mouth. Luckily, I was interrupted by my phone buzzing. Seeing it was Chase calling, I answered.

"What's good?"

He was inquiring on how things went with the tip on Candace.

"Oh, I saw the bitch... scared the piss outta her today. I'm on that bitch though, trust me." We chopped it up about some other shit then ended the call.

"Now, back to bed. Maybe you're tired, little bro."

"So you're working your way back to the pen? You just can't stay away, huh?" JU said.

I turn my nose up at the nigga. "What the fuck you talking about?"

"You know what I'm talking about! The bitch...you found her-what now? You gone get rid of her and get caught up in a new charge?"

"Slow down, young bull," I said, dusting my Burberry V-neck sweater off, regretting getting black instead of gray. "I'm not going back to prison, and I'm not in the business of getting rid of people, either. What you need to worry about is keeping your ass out of the line of fire! I stay out of jail and you stay out of the claws of grimy bitches and hungry niggas."

He turned his attention back to the TV. Maybe that shit was kind of harsh. I'm guessing he calls himself loving that bitch. After the awkward silence, we were able to break the ice and watch the game together. I made a promise I intended on keeping. I wasn't going back to jail-not now, not ever.

CHAPTER 15

The Hand I Was Dealt

LONDON

The judge wasn't as bad as I thought. She called damn near every case, leaving mine for last. That alone had me shook, thinking I was going to do a 5-year bid, for sure.

"State your name for the record," Judge Braxton said.

She had me confirm I understood everything she was reading off, but honestly, I stopped listening after awhile. I was just waiting for her to determine my fate. When the lawyer asked for he and the Prosecutor to approach the bench, my fucking stomach started hurting! All the whispering had me nauseous as fuck... By the time she read all the charges were dismissed for lack of evidence, I couldn't hear shit! I felt a gush of something running down my leg. I look down to see nothing but blood... I passed out...

LEAH

The house was coming together. I was waiting for UPS call saying my baby bed had arrived, then it would be just about that time. I was so fucking excited and nervous at the same time. Jonathan was in his room watching TV and I was painting little Moe's room. I decided I wanted another son. Men loved boys because they got to mold a mini him. Everything about Moe was fine. Even his feet looked good. This baby had to be damn near perfect to match Moe and me, because we definitely looked good together.

Damn, I almost forgot I needed to call the realtor! I had a couple questions about the paperwork. I searched everywhere for that sheet thinking I must have left it at work. Shit! As nosy as those women were, I needed not leave shit laying around for them to find. I was floating on cloud nine when I felt a sudden episode coming on. I ran upstairs and locked myself in the bathroom. "Not again!" I cried, hoping Jonathan would stay far away from me

CHAPTER 16

Never Loved You More

DEANNA

Came home from work and Moe was sitting in the living room shouting at the basketball game on TV. After removing my shoes and coat, I walked over greeting him with a kiss on the cheek. He looked over for a split second.

"How was your day, baby?" he asked.

"My day was cool. I was just ready to go, as usual." We both laughed! He informed me that he had just run me some bath water, so it should still be hot. "Aww, thanks baby, that's perfect!" I said, stripping outta my clothes in a rush to get in the tub. "I'm gonna go relax while you finish watching your crap…" I closed the bathroom door, lit a candle and climbed in. Fresh bubbles and the water were just how I like it. I hit the playlist on my phone to listen to August Alsina's, *Kissin' On My Tattoos.*

Baby I don't blame you...for being in the club, getting all that love
'Cause you're so beautiful
God made you to show that off
Now I ain't ever been the jealous type of guy
But I want you to myself, I can't lie
I know we ain't on no one on one thing
But baby, it should change
'Cause when I be out with other chicks I be thinking 'bout you
And when you be out on dates you be texting me too
Telling me to come pick you up when he drop you off
I pray to God he ain't breaking you off….

I closed my eyes to relax…

I stayed in a little over an hour listening to music. Once out, I dried off and wrapped myself in a fresh towel. "Where is my robe?" I thought to myself. I made my way to the living room with Moe.

I peeked over his shoulder…

"I guess you ain't shrivel up and die in there, huh?" he said.

We both laughed… "Shut up!" I yelled.

"Go grab that baby oil gel out the closet."

"Awww, shoot!" I said, excited, knowing I was about to get that rub down I loved so much. His hands were so relaxing and strong... I retrieved the oil and headed back.

****

MOE

My dick instantly got rock hard staring at my wife laying across my lap on her stomach. I started to toss the oil like, "fuck this," and get right down to business, but I wanted her body relaxed.

I started with all the pressure points first. Starting with the back of her neck where her spine meets the skull, I used my fingertips, slowly increasing the pressure here and there. Her body literally felt like it was melting in my hands. I massaged her perfect round ass, closing my own eyes, enjoying the feeling, too. I lifted her up, stood to my feet and laid her back on the square ottoman in the middle of the floor. I got down on my knees, immediately caressing her pussy with my tongue. She moaned, throwing her legs around my neck making sure I didn't move. I had no intentions of stopping until she was screaming for more. When she came, it was so hard and uncontrollable, I damn near shot my nut by the sound of hers. I knew if I didn't move fast, it would be too late... I flipped her over, massaging her ass again while I entered her from the back

"Fuckkkkk!!!" I yelled, throwing my head back. She was dripping wet. Closing my eyes, I tried to concentrate on anything but the feeling of her walls clamped down on me, forcing me to move stronger and faster... Fucking her from the back always got the best of me, and this time was no different. I couldn't say a word or even get a moan out. I clinched my teeth together, spread her ass and fucked her, sending both us over the edge. I laughed to myself, remembering doggy style used to be her least favorite position. Now she throwing her ass like a pro.

She still felt like paradise. Laying next to my girl made me realize everything I needed was right here. I still feel fucked up about everything. I never wanted to hurt her, not ever in life. I stroked her back while she slept...making mental notes of her breathing, her cheekbones, just everything, all the way down to the curve of her back. Those things alone made me realize I never wanted to be without her. This secret was for the best. I planted a baby inside her! At least I was hoping I did. It was time, and in my mind, when the shit hit the fan, I would need something that would attach me to her. I knew how DeAnna felt about family, and she wouldn't cut me out the picture if a baby was smack in the middle. Leah was damn near about to drop, and without something for her to call her own, it was like killing her twice. I was gon' try again if last night didn't work. I didn't know how much longer I had, but I would die before I let my baby go away from me.

CHAPTER 17

Bloodshed

CANDACE

It was time to make my move. I took one last look at the
shitty motel, feeling somewhat relieved everything was about
to be behind me. If I could just shake this eerie feeling that
came over me after thinking I saw Jasper at the gas station,
I'd be okay. Once inside the cab, I let out a sigh of relief.

"Where to, ma'am?"

"The Greyhound station." He pulled off and headed
downtown. It was a little congested on Grand River Ave., so

when he turned down the side street, I didn't think anything of it. "Thirty minutes until departure," I said to myself, still trying hard to calm my nerves. About two blocks down from the station, the driver pulled over. "Umm, hello...we have two more blocks," I said, pointing ahead.

"I'm sorry, ma'am, this is the farthest I'm going...this is your stop."

"What do you mean? I'm paying you to take me to the bus station, not a side street. What kind of shit is that?" I snapped.

"This is your stop!" he repeated.

I snatched my purse from the seat. "How much do I owe you?"

"It's paid for."

The hair on the back of my neck stood straight up. Paid for? That made me suddenly look around in a panic.

He said over his shoulder, "I have to go now," hitting the button to unlock the doors.

I hurried, snatching my backpack and purse, then rushed out the cab and up the first block.

I glanced over my shoulder several times, feeling like someone was behind me, but no one was there. I was almost at the end of the block when someone wearing all black with a hooded silhouette stepped out from the shadows. I looked at the distance to the bus station-I'd never make it! I thought about screaming, but that was probably pointless, too. I had nowhere to run, nowhere to hide; this was my last stop like the driver said. I dropped my bag on the ground when I saw the barrel of the gun pointing at me. I closed my eyes for the last time.

JASPER

It was pitch fucking black out here, just me and the glow from the end of this ninety dollar Habana. I'd been waiting on the right occasion to fire this bitch up and enjoy it. Nothing like a few quiet moments waiting to catch a dirt bag bitch... I sat back and watched the shit play out. In between thoughts, briefly, my mind flashed back to that encounter with DeAnna at her place. Not now, though. I redirected my thoughts-first things first. A smile spread across my lips. "Checkmate," I said, watching two blows to the head and the body dropping to the ground. I kept my promise to little baby bro. I said I wouldn't murk the bitch and I didn't! I pulled off slowly, bending a few corners, waiting for the car to pull up. "Damn, little mama, you almost made my dick hard!" I said, joking to ole girl. She completed the job with that,

' FUCK ME...NO...FUCK YOU!" type attitude that I liked. "Little mama a stone cold killer," I thought to myself, giving her an approving nod. I passed Samantha the envelope filled with the ticket payment. She was 20GS heavier, easy.

"I gotta take this call. Lose my number," I said, getting the fuck on.

"Yo! What's good?" I said, answering the phone.

I listened in on an update I wasn't prepared for. "Are you sure?" I questioned, hoping I wasn't hearing the shit right. "Yeah, thanks for the info baby…" How fucked up was this shit!

"JU, where you at bro?" I said through the car radio.

"Home, why?" JU said.

"I'm on my way to get you. Be ready…" I hung up. I wasn't ready to explain and I couldn't give up too much info, anyway. This call right here just change the whole fucking game!

CHAPTER 18

Looking Crazy

OMAR

I walked through the front entrance of the hospital and sat on the bench. I hadn't been back since my father died. I wanted to go and apologize to DeAnna for not listening to what she had to say about Candace and tell her about what happened in NC. Sighing, I walked to the information desk to ask that they page DeAnna so she could come down. I waited for about 20 minutes and she never showed. "Maybe she doesn't work on Tuesdays…" I thought to myself, trying to remember her old schedule. I thought about going up to the floor and looking for her but decided against that. I'll just come back tomorrow…

I was waiting on Valet to bring my car back around when I saw Genie, DeAnna's nurse friend. I greeted her and told her I just got back in to town and I was looking for DeAnna . She hesitated at first, but I guess felt the need to tell me that she was back with her husband after having a terrible accident. She seemed like she wanted to tell me more, but said she needed to respect her privacy and her marriage. After all he put her through she went back to him? I shook my head in disbelief, not wanting to accept the reality that what I had with her was over. I left the hospital alone and obviously, what I thought was meant for me already belonged to someone else…

CHAPTER 19

A Love Of My Own

LONDON

"Relax, Miss Green, you won't feel the cutting or pain," the nurse said. "Possibly some pressure or sensations, but with the medicine coming through your IV, you should be fine."

"What's wrong? Why do you have to cut him out? Can't I push?"

"I'm sorry, sweetheart, with all of your complications, it's safer this way to get in and get him out. We want you awake so you can see your boy."

I was high as shit. Thankfully, I couldn't feel anything like she'd said, just a whole lot of tugging and moving around. "I wish you were here, baby," I said silently to myself, thinking of JU. Never in a million years did I think I'd be lying on a table awaiting the arrival of a baby. I always thought De would go first. I heard crying, then everyone was smiling and the Doctor said, "There he is."

They cut his cord and laid him on my chest. He was so small, I was scared to touch him.

"Congratulations, mom! It's okay, he won't break." the nurse said.

Slowly, I wrapped my arm around him and rubbed his hair. The crying stopped instantly. "Hey, Saint... hey, mommy son..." Tears of joy and pain ran down my face. My baby was here, safe in my arms. Thank you, God...

JU

"What was the rush?" I asked Jasper as he dipped in and out of traffic, driving fast as hell down Woodward Ave. We almost hit two fucking cars running the lights and shit. "Bro, are you gon' tell me what the problem is? Is it Ma?" I asked. He looked over at me. "Nah. Ma good." Jas said, still avoiding the question.

"Look man, I was doing what I was supposed to do...just know that!" he said, whipping into Hutzel Hospital's valet area.

He hopped out quick.

"Come on bro, hurry up!" Jasper demanded.

We walked up to the security desk and they asked who we were here to see. Jasper looked at me and said, "Lil bro I'll explain everything when we get a chance alright?"

He turned to security and said "He here to see London Green!" and he walked back out the hospital revolving doors.

"What nigga?" I said, following behind Jasper, not feeling this sick ass game he playing. "Sir, she's on the 4ᵗʰ floor in room 413."

I looked at the door again just as Jasper pulled off and then back at the security guard. I grabbed the pass, unaware that my life would officially be changed forever in a matter of moments.

I got off the elevator in search of the room. My nerves were fucked up as I stood outside the door. When I walked in, I could see someone in the bed, but with their back facing the door. I walked around to the other side and stood there…

It was her…London! I couldn't do shit but stand there waiting for the cameras to roll in and announce I was being Punk'd. I had to be, because this was some sick ass shit. She opened her eyes, her face matching my expression like a clone.

"JU," she called out, cuffing her mouth with her hand,

surprised.

I paced back and forth scratching my head. "What the FUCK?" I shouted, wanting to knock some shit over. A nurse came running in, but London interrupted her questioning, informing her that everything was okay. She walked back out closing the door behind her.

"How is this possible?" I said with my back turned to her. "You were dead. Your neighbor…" I just stopped fighting the lump that formed in my throat.

'The last thing I want you to do is think that I would harm you." She said softly. "I'm not the person your brother thinks I am, JU. I promise you that."

I listened, still making her to speak to my back while I took everything in. I didn't know what the fuck to believe anymore. It's like living a fuckin' nightmare, but I'm not sleep. Was I hearing her right? Every couple of minutes I would pinch the inside of my arm to be sure I wasn't dreaming this shit. I had to be losing my fucking mind. "So, you just been laying in this hospital bed all this time and didn't think to contact me and say shit about nothing?"

"I've been in jail JU! You know I would've called you if I could," London said.

"So, they stopped making pay phones in jail, too?" I snapped.

"I didn't know what he told you and if you believed any of

it. It was safer for me and Saint in that cell, anyway."

I turned around, finally facing her… "Who the fuck is Saint? Your set-up partna?" I spat.

"No JU! There's so much we need to talk about. I just don't know where to start."

"How about you start with the truth?"

CHAPTER 20

Snatched

LEAH

Now would be a perfect time, if any, to make my move. I walked in for my regular shift as normal as possible. My heart was racing, my mind fixated on not leaving this hospital today without my baby. I waited long enough- this would be around the time I was due to give birth. I didn't want Moe speculating that anything was fishy about my pregnancy, seeing as how I haven't seen him the whole way through. I saw the perfect baby; he was beautiful. His complexion was a handsome caramel... His eyes were green like an emerald, his head full of curls. He was perfect! After counting all fingers and toes, I made up my mind that he would be the chosen one. After carefully investigating my exit, I was confident I'd get away.

I stared down at the duct tape, hoping I didn't have to put this over his little mouth. I'd watched him for days. He didn't seem to be much of a crier. I prepared my cart and headed to the Mom and Baby unit to get my son. I peered through all the doors until I got to the nursery. I made sure it was after feeding time so that the little one would be asleep. "Ok, Leah…it's game time," I said to myself. Smiling, I knocked on the door.

She's coming…

"Good morning," the nurse said.

My heart was beating so damn fast. I glanced over at my son for a split second as I headed to the bathroom and started cleaning. I was just about done. The two nurses were at the desk talking, so neither of them saw when I unplugged the monitor on one of the babies. All types of alarms went off. I watched both of them rushing over to the incubator to see what the problem was… I hurried to my cart, pulling out the fake silicone baby I purchased online weeks ago, already wrapped in a hospital receiving blanket. After one last look at the nurses, I switched the babies, then placed my son in the cart just as the nurse realized the shit was unplugged. "Have a nice day, ladies," I said, hurrying out while they were running checks. I moved cautiously through the halls, heading straight for the elevator. I was almost there...

"Ma'am, ma'am, excuse me, can I grab some of the towels from your cart?" the guy asked.

Shit! "If you hit your call button, someone can bring you some. These in this cart have to go back," I lied. He reached in the cart to grab a towel, anyway. I slid my hand inside my pockets, clutching my scissors.

"This will do!" he said, walking away.

I pressed the button to the elevator, praying no one else attempted to stop me. My patience was worn thin at this point.

Finally in the basement, I pushed the cart inside the morgue. This was a foolproof plan. I needed to get my baby out of here and *fast*. I opened up the freezer and removed a body that already had the internal organs removed. I carefully placed my snuggly wrapped baby into the stomach of the cadaver and zipped the body bag. Now, I'm ready to change. I removed the next outfit from the bottom of the trash bin on the housekeeping cart-all black suit with long black trench coat, a black fedora hat, and some blacked-out sunglasses. My heart began to beat even faster with the joy of knowing my baby was soon to be home with me. I rolled the gurney right down the hall and out the door as others looked on, none the wiser.

CHAPTER 21

Lose Control

MOE

Just when I got shit going good with Deanna, here come this muthafucka trying to fuck it up. I'm not gon' let nothing come between us this time; this my wife & Im lucky enough to have a second chance with her. I laid next to her, watching her sleep. "Damn, she so beautiful," I thought to myself. I see her phone going off and the number not saved. "You do something to me every time I see you, girl. I can't wait to have you in my presence, tonight." What the fuck? I read the message over five times before flipping the fuck out. How this nigga texting her? I purposely blocked his number. And what the fuck he mean every time he see her? So, she been out with this nigga? I need answers NOW.

"Aye, who the fuck you been going out with?" I yelled, waking her up. "What you talking about?" she asked, groggy and confused.

"Who the fuck is this talking about he can't wait to see you tonight?" I tossed the phone at her. She read the message looking dumb. "Oh, so you don't know…" I was so fucking mad. Not only was she talking to him before but she lost her memory, but somehow still ended up talking to this nigga? Something ain't right. Then I thought about Amber slick ass… she probably had him introduce himself like a brand new nigga. "I don't know who this is, Moe." I knew she wasn't lying. I forgot she lost her memory for a second. She wouldn't have a reason to go behind my back because she don't remember shit I did. Imma deal with Amber shady ass. I told her to mind her fucking business, and the fact that I just seen this nigga, then he had the audacity to text my wife? Had my blood *boiling*. "It's probably just a wrong number my bad," I said, playing it cool. She turned over going back to sleep. "Imma have to kill this nigga," I thought to myself.

LONDON

I had JU wheel me to the Nursery, anticipating what he'd do when he saw our son. I'm guessing he didn't pay attention that this was the baby unit, but that was even better. "Pull up to the door on the right," I said. I hit the buzzer, and the nurse came. "He needs a wristband," I informed her. "Congratulations to you, too, sir!" she said, flashing her white teeth. "I'll go get him."

JU leaned down in front of me, bending his knees to be at eye level.

"Get the fuck out of here..." he said.

I gave a nod, confirming his thoughts were correct. "Saint is his name, baby." I saw him rubbing his cheek...I had been longing to touch him since the moment he walked in the room. His eyes filled up with tears...

"We have a son?" he whispered, looking directly in my eyes.

"When I was at court..." I was cut off by the sound of sirens with blinking red lights. "Code pink! Code pink!" shouted the voice on the intercom. Doors around us started slammimg as security and hospital staff started rushing through the halls.

"Damn, what's going on?" JU wondered.

Just then, I noticed Jasper getting off the elevator. The

nurse returned, asking that we go back to my room immediately. "OK, that's fine. Just hand me my son, and I'll take him back with me." I'm done resting.

"Miss Green, I'm sorry, there's been some type of problem. I went to scan the baby bracelet to add dad to him, but he's not in the crib."

"What problem? What are you talking about? Go get my fucking son right now!"

"Miss Green, please calm down." she said.

"Don't tell her to calm down. Where's my son?" JU questioned.

She was trying to explain, but I could tell she was scared to death. She was stuttering and looking at everyone running through the hallways.

"What's going on?" Jasper chimed in.

I used my right hand to guard the staples across my stomach area and slowly stood as both JU and the Nurse stepped up, grabbing my arms to assist me. I stared Jasper square in the eyes. "Where the fuck is my son?" I said, barely above a whisper.

"Who you talking to?" Jasper replied.

I stepped closer to him...

"You had me fucked up then, and you got me fucked up now. I know your kind...secretly jealous of your little brother because he's everything you are not," I said, pointing my finger dead in his face.

JU stepped in between us, placing his hand on Jasper's chest, pushing him back out of my reach.

I looked at JU.

"What, is this all a sick fucking joke you coming here pretending you didn't know I just delivered a baby? How did you even know I was here?"

He looked at Jasper....

"What did you do, Jasper?"

CHAPTER 22

Vexed

JU

I didn't know what the fuck to believe anymore. It's like living a fuckin' nightmare, but I'm not sleep. Was I hearing this nigga right? He sitting here explaining to me how he had eyes on London the whole time yet he left me to believe she was dead? "How fucking sick are you?" I shouted at Jasper.

"Look bro, I don't expect for you to understand moves I make cause you ain't cut like me. But hear this: my intentions are always good, fam! You almost fuckin' died, bro!" he yelled. "You ain't see the look on Mama face watching you on tubes and shit, nigga. Fuck yo feelin's behind that bitch."

Without any hesitation I went dead in his shit! I swung so hard I damn near lost my balance. Jasper tackled me to the floor in a rage, grabbed me by my neck and pulled his arm back ready to hit me. I waited... I didn't give a fuck at this point... but he didn't hit me. In fact, he got up and walked out the door, slamming it. I couldn't move. I felt like I was in shock or something like it. My son was missing and London blamed US! She had to know better... but then again, the way she was treated, why would she think positive when it came to this? I was gon' find Saint, no matter what was at cost, and if Jasper had anything to do with it... I planned on cutting him off forever.

CHAPTER 23

No Stone Left Unturned

JASPER

I ain't owe that bitch no explanation, but JU was another story. It fucked me up that he really questioned my involvement with the kidnapping of my own damn nephew… He knows how I feel about him, hell, my family period-his son would be one in the same. If something happened to either of them, I'd never be able to live with myself. I'd die before I let anything happen to them.

I looked in my rearview to check my eye. "That nigga got a mean right hook," I thought to myself, looking at the swelling. I started to beat his little ass, but I get it. I phoned

Chase to be on standby. I was headed to the hospital to ask some questions, 'cause somebody knew something. This wild ass girl has done so much, there's no telling what she has JU and this baby caught up in. Lucky for her, this shit just became my problem, as well. Anything with my blood attached meant all-out war.

Swiftly, I walked through the halls back to that nurses station. I wanted names of any and every person that was on shift from the time she delivered up until he went missing. "Excuse me," I said, getting the receptionist's attention as I looked around. All giddy and shit, she looked up smiling.

"Heyyy, can I help you?" she asked.

"I'm hoping you can…I need a list of everyone that works in this unit." She looked confused.

"I'm sorry, exactly what do you need?"

With both hands, I rubbed my freshly shaved beard managing to pull together a smile.

"Ok, it's kind of private information in regards to my family." I pulled a stack from the inside pocket of my black Shearling coat, slapping it on the station. "Listen baby, my nephew went missing a couple days ago from this floor and nobody seems to know when or how." She was all ears and now it was her looking over her shoulder and around for anyone who could possibly overhear our conversation. I glanced down at her badge…

"Veronica, if you could give me any information, I'd gladly make it worth the trouble." She got up from the chair...

"Give me a second, but I need you to go down to the lounge, alright?" she said.

I was cautious at first, not knowing if the woman was trying to go alert somebody, but I really ain't have a choice.... I waited about 10 minutes, ready to go back again when she came rushing up the hall signaling for me to follow her in the staff restroom door. Once in she gave me some information. She stated she didn't know if this was a hunch or what but I could see where it took me. She said she felt something fishy about the girl that was volunteering on their floor. She told me about how she was always looking and acting weird, and basically, very standoffish. She told me she was here the day the baby went missing and how crazy everyone thought it was that something like that could happen.

"She left this paper one day with an address on it...you can check it out." she said.

"Have you seen her since that day?" I asked.

"Nope, that's the thing-I was already suspicious before the baby incident, but that sealed it for me!" Veronica said.

"Who else have you told this to?" I asked, wondering if the bitch was a blabber mouth, which I figured she was the way she was running shit down right now.

"No one, just you. Police have been all up and through

here questioning all of us. I feel so sorry for that mother."

"Well, look, here's the bread. I'd appreciate if you didn't mention this to anybody else." She handed me her number saying if I had any more questions to text her. I left immediately, ready to meet Chase and check this address out.

CHASE

"What the fuck kind of shit is this?" Jasper said.

We both looked at the boarded-up house that sat on a dead-end street. "This bitch is sick," I said. "You sure this the crib?"

"Yeah, that's what ole girl said." Jas handed me the piece of paper with an address on it.

"Alright bro, give me a minute. I'll be right back." Jas got out and climbed in the driver seat to back the shooter in the alley next to her house.

I walked around the back of the house looking for entry. This bitch had this muthafuckin' door locked; I couldn't even tell how she was getting in and out. I got tired of walking back and forth looking and shit. I screwed the silencer on my Eagle to suppress the noise and walked up to the back door. *Psss, psss...* I fired two shots into the frame, blowing the lock, making a hole in the back door. Gun in hand, moving swiftly through the back of the house, I searched for the baby.

BINGO! I found her sleep in bed with the baby in her arms. I walked slowly up to the bed until I towered over both of them. I placed the barrel of the Glock in the middle of her forehead and applied pressure. Her eyes flew open! She tried to pull the baby into her chest. A devilish grin spread across my face as I applied more pressure behind the gun. "Nah, this what you gone do... roll yo ass away from the baby and face that way," I said, pointing to the wall behind her. When she hesitated, I told the bitch if I had to repeat myself, her brains would meet the wall, instead. She softly slid her arms from under the baby and began to roll over toward the wall. I gently grabbed JU's son and cradled him on my side. As planned, I sent the message to Jas and he rushed right in. For a split second, my nigga looked like he was gone shed some tears. I passed the baby over and told Jas to go.

"Give me my baby back!" she rolled over and shouted.

Without words, Jas pulled the burner and aimed at her head! "Don't shoot dog... the baby..." I quickly said. "Go bro, I got it- trust me." He looked at me then back to her... "Torture that bitch, bro. Make that bitch suffer."

LEAH

I couldn't feel anything. I tried to move, but it was like my brain wasn't connecting to the rest of my body. Excruciating pain shot through my side as I tried to stand, forcing me to collapse back across the floor.

The noises started again…

…laughter from my mother:

Hush little baby don't say a word…momma's gonna buy you a mockingbird.

And if that mockingbird don't sing…momma's gonna buy you a diamond ring

If that diamond ring don't shineeee…momma's gonna sing you a lullaby…

I lay still waiting on the noise to stop but it never did. I remember my in case of emergency stash spots that were hiding around. I managed to crawl over to the night stand, pulling a knife from out of the bottom drawer. I didn't know if he was still in the house or coming back to finish me off. I crawled behind the door and lay there hiding, hoping for this nightmare to be over…

CHAPTER 24

Mayhem

LONDON

I pushed the back door open slowly and crept inside. My heart was beating so fast I could hardly catch my breath. I was focused... I walked up the small flight of steps, ready for whatever. It didn't look like anybody was home... I abruptly stopped in my tracks... I reached for the photograph that sat on the fireplace ledge....

What the fuck?? My adrenaline began to rush. I stared at the infant who had an identical birthmark like the one Saint had on his left thigh resembling a clover. I grabbed the next frame, suddenly feeling sick to my fucking stomach. A picture of that bitch, Leah who Moe was fucking with her fucking titty popped in my baby's mouth feeding him...I damn near lost it! Rage took over, and I didn't give a fuck who was here, or what I had to do.

Swiftly, I headed up the flight of stairs walking into a nursery. I was tripping! Did this bitch plan this? The blood splattered on the walls, across the bed and all over the carpet had me frozen. In a state of shock, I crept over to the baby bed leaning in, but nothing was there....to my left behind the door I saw the body of a woman. I walked over bending down to roll her over. I didn't even see the knife coming before see stabbed me, causing me to fall. She tried to jump on top of me, but I swung, striking her in the face. We both managed to get off the floor.

"Where the fuck is my baby, bitch?" This time, we both delivered blows, swinging non-stop. Leah backed up to charge at me, but I moved out of the way, causing Leah to run head-first into the wood of the crib, knocking her out.

I began to cough severely, feeling as though I couldn't breathe. Clutching my throat, I fell to the floor, noticing smoke coming from the vents. Oh, my God, the house is on fire...I didn't have any more fight left. My blood loss caused me to feel faint... I could feel my lungs swelling up. I thought about Saint… I would never get to touch him, hold him, kiss his innocent face. With all the strength I had, I started crawling around the room. "Where are you, baby?" Black smoke was filling the room. I was losing air! The last thing I remember seeing was JU's handsome face before my eyes closed….

JU

Bro wasn't as slick as he thought. I knew all of his information, so I called the phone company and had them transfer his number to mine. I was getting all the messages and everything. I pulled up at the address he shot Chase, but it looked like a vacant house. I would've kept going, but I saw smoke coming from the back which made me curious. I walked up the side of the house to the back following the smoke. The door was open. I covered my face with my hat and took my chances on going in. If they thought my son could've been here, I was damn sho gon' go in to see. "Damn, somebody does live here…" I said, confused about why the outside was boarded up. I heard coughing coming from upstairs. I moved fast, not wanting to get caught in a burning ass house. "London!" I howled, seeing her body lying on the floor as soon as I reached the top landing. I dialed 911 in case something happened that was out of my control. I tried to pick her up, but the smoke was so fucking thick, I started coughing, too. I heard sirens. "Thank God," I said. "Hang on, baby. They coming." I laid on top of her, trying to block the smoke from her body as much as I could.

DEANNA

I was so happy to be back to feeling normal again. I missed all my little work buddies at my job and serving patients, too. "My office needs dusting..." I thought as I looked. It felt so bizarre that I had been off a whole month. Moe's ass obviously needed a break from me, too, and just didn't want to admit it. We've been great lately! He's been so devoted to making sure everything is pretty much perfect in our world. Last night was so crazy, though. He went ape shit about a text message from some dude who clearly had the wrong damn number. I don't recall ever seeing him that damn mad. He scared me...

My day was moving slow thanks to Genie taking half my patient load. I keep telling everyone I'm fine but no one seems to listen.

I stared down at the pamphlet in the top drawer of my desk. Confused, I flipped through the pages reading some of the material. "That's strange...I don't recall ever having this here." I tossed it in the trash, as it wasn't something I needed.

I still hadn't heard from London and was starting to get worried…

TRAUMA TEAM TO AMBULANCE ENTRANCE…
"Finally, some excitement!" I thought to myself…

I jumped up, grabbing my stethoscope and running to the entrance. I lived for this stuff.

We all stood at the door waiting for the EMS to pull up. Genie was looking over all the equipment making sure we were prepared and ready to go. "What was the call?" I asked Genie.

"Female badly beaten with multiple body fractures and smoke inhalation," she replied.

As soon as the van backed in, we got to work. We were transferring her from the stretcher to the bed when I got a look at her face. My goodness…this was the chick I saw last week outside the garage talking to Moe! I kept working, unsure why I kept seeing this woman, thinking this was one hell of a coincidence. "Leah Thomas must have really pissed someone off to do this to her," the doctor said.

Leah Thomas I repeated in my head…nope, didn't ring a bell.

There were eight of us in the room running around. This was one thing I loved about Receiving Trauma team-it's always all hands on deck. We stabilized her.

"Great job, team," Doc said, as some of us walked out the

room.

Another call came through… "What the hell?" I said, looking at Genie. Guess our day just got interesting… Genie ran back to the ambulance entrance to receive the next trauma coming in. I headed to the room to prep. I overheard that this one was a female stab victim with smoke inhalation as well. They must have been together. What are the odds of that?

I heard them coming down the hall, and I was ready!

"DeAnna! DeAnna!" I heard Genie calling out…

Terror was written all over her face! The pushed the stretcher in and instantly I saw London and lost it!

"We know the rules: no family allowed on staff. Get her out of here." Doc said.

"No, Doc, noooo! I'm okay, please let me stay with her." I saw them cut her shirt open. She had staples across her abdomen.

"Doc, victim has a fresh c-section incision that has reopened with lots of bleeding," one of the staff members called out.

"WHAT???" I shouted.

"GET HER OUT!" Doc said again.

Kicking and screaming, I was removed from the room in total disbelief.

CHAPTER 25

Memory Lane

DEANNA

"What happened to her?" I cried as Genie rubbed my back. I was so angry they wouldn't allow me in the room with London. I'd never been so scared in my life. I sat in my office terrified, jumping each time I saw somebody walk past the door. After about 10 minutes or so, I jumped up and headed back down to the room. They were gonna have to arrest me, fire me, or something, 'cause I was going back in there with my cousin-she needed me. I don't know if I got up too fast or what, but I felt dizzy like the floor was moving. I stopped and leaned against the wall. This excruciating headache came outta nowhere.

I stood there holding my head. I walked up a little further thinking maybe I should sit down. I heard what sounded like Moe's voice coming from the room on the right. Barely able to see through squinted eyes due to the debilitating pain, I thought my eyes were playing tricks on me. Flashes of memories flooded my head. I closed my eyes and leaned against the wall again, waiting for it to stop, then it did! He didn't see me but I saw him sitting there with that woman.

Why didn't I know this before? I must have suffered some type of memory loss, as I was remembering I crashed onto the expressway. This nigga was playing on me the whole time knowing damn well we weren't together. All of them lied! I ran to my office to grab my purse. I needed to get the hell outta there. I bumped into Genie on the way out.

"Are you leaving, babe?" she asked.

I gave her the evil eye, surprised she would even go along with such a thing. I didn't have to say anything. The look on her face indicated she knew I was back. I stormed out that hospital running dead smack into Jasper. Wow... I recalled the most recent memory of him as well. Funny thing is as it replays, he was trying to tell me. He just stood there, looking just as lost as I was. "Get me outta here," I said to him with tears in my eyes. He turned around, opened the door for me to get in, and we pulled off.

"Where to, baby?" he asked.

"Far away from here."

MOE

I grabbed the bitch by the throat, squeezing down. I caught myself, remembering the doctor had just seen me in here. Remembering some shit I saw on CSI, I thought fast. I saw a needle the nurse must've left by mistake laying on the tray next to the sink. Without any hesitation, I snatched it up and walked back over to the bed. Now she was looking dead in my face. "This is the fastest flight to hell you could ever be granted, you lying bitch." I screwed the syringe onto her IV and forced 30cc of air like it was done on the show. She started looking and moving like she was choking or some shit. Leah was reaching for me but I stood away from her and watched while she was gargling blood and all. "Fuck you, bitch," I said, watching her eyes roll up into her head.

CHAPTER 26

LAST BREATH

Final chapter

LONDON

Life has a crazy way of showing you how easily things could fall apart. In such a short time, everything I thought I knew had changed. I never stopped praying the whole way through. I kept faith that God would forgive me my sins and allow me a second chance.

"How you feeling Ms. Green?" asked the nurse.

I just kept staring at the ceiling wanting to say terrible, but I settled for a hand gesture to say, "so-so."

"You have someone dying to see you," she said, smiling extremely hard.

It has to be DeAnna. By now, someone had called her to tell her what went down with everything. How could I tell my cousin that I had lost my son by the hands of the same bitch who ruined her life? I was ashamed. The nurse walked out and I closed my eyes again, hoping to just lay here and die.

"There she is, Saint," a familiar voice said.

Opening my eyes to see JU standing there holding our son almost killed me. I shot up in the bed blinking fast, hoping this wasn't a dream. The sound of my son crying instantly brought me to tears. I briefly looked at JU, who had tears running down his face, too.

'How did…" I couldn't even get the words out, I was so choked up. I stuck my arms out and reached for my baby.

"Jasper found him. How did you know where to go?" JU said.

"I went back up to the hospital 'cause the cops wanted to ask some questions to see if I could assist them in the search with any information. I was down there for about 3 hours… on my way out, I was bumped by this lady on the elevator, knocking my purse on the floor. Because of the life I've lived, the things I've done, I found it strange that she bumped into me that hard like that, but I thought I was just tripping. When I got to the exit, I remembered the face of the lady in the elevator. She was one of the nurses on shift when Saint was kidnapped. I reached in my pocket to pull out the card of the officer over the case when a piece of paper fell out my pocket. I stared at it, not remembering it being there before. Then it hit me: I wasn't off at all. The shit in the elevator was on purpose. She must have seen me and remembered who I was. I didn't stop and go back to question the shit, either. Nothing happens by chance.

I really didn't care who, what, or why… all I cared about was my son being in my arms." JU gently passed Saint to me, but he didn't back away. He walked to the other side of the bed and climbed in next to me, wiping the tears from my eyes. I couldn't stop crying. God heard me! He forgave me for everything I'd done and He spared my son. For awhile, we just laid there taking it all in…we had a baby. I looked over at JU, not knowing where to start. I knew he had so many questions.

"I was never gonna do it," I said, looking directly into his eyes. "I swear on my life, from the moment I saw you, I had made my mind up I wouldn't. You have to believe me, JU." He sat there for a minute silent.

"Let me ask you something…who is Jason?" JU asked.

I looked down at Saint and kissed his lips softly before answering…"Jason was my best friend."

He raised his brows as if to say, "*--and keep going.*"

"I didn't know he wanted to be with me; we've always been friends-since we were kids. He taught me how to hustle and make money. Everything was good until I met you!" I remember what Callie said about not going into details, just hitting the basics and keeping it as simple as I could. "Yes, I set niggas up, but I told him I wanted out for good and I feel he got mad and decided to do it himself. I would have never let that happen to you..."

MOE

I got the fuck on quick before anybody else could enter the room to find the bitch body. I was moving as normal as I could, trying not to draw attention to myself. I was about to hit the steps when that lady Genie called my name. "Fuck," I said under my breath. "What's up?" I asked.

"She knows."

"She knows what?" I asked, already irritated with her holding me up and shit. She went on to tell me the shit that happened with London and how all the emotions must have triggered something in DeAnna, 'cause the next time she saw her, she was furious.

"She looked at me with so much anger...I've never seen her like that before."

"Where did she go?" I started to panic...

"I chased her almost to the door and she jumped in the car with some guy," she said, dropping her head.

I knew then there was only one thing to do. I walked away from Genie mid-sentence, pulling out my phone and dialing the number I saw in hers, praying I was wrong.

"Yo," the nigga spat in the phone.

"You got my wife with you, nigga?" I asked, lip turned up in a stiff scowl. I stood in the middle of the lobby waiting on a response. "You being followed right now, muthafucka," I spat. He laughed!

The phone hung up and I received a video call from DeAnna. "Thank God," I said out loud. I accepted the call, but the face on the screen wasn't De.

"Take a picture, muthafucka! Make sure whoever, if ever you send a nigga at me, you show my face. This same face gone be the last one you see when I murk yo ass, lil homie." He hung up.

I rushed home to grab my pistol and go find his tuff ass. DeAnna must didn't tell this nigga who he was fucking with.

DEANNA

This isn't real. This can't be happening. You have to wake up, you're dreaming. This isn't real. This can't be happening. You have to wake up, you're dreaming.

How did I get here? I lay wrapped up in the arms of a man I barely know seeking comfort. As he blankets me cry…with each tear I shed, I recall another memory of Moe breaking my heart into a million pieces.

"I got you baby girl," Jasper said as he stroked my back.

I felt safe here. I felt loved here. Why did I still feel like I was doing something wrong? I wanted so much to go back and face everything that happened, but another part of me wanted to say fuck it all. Although his hands felt good and promising, there was nothing he could do to make me feel better. I sat up and looked at him for a moment, then leaned down and kissed his lips. I thanked him for trying. I wanted to stay right here forever, but I knew that wasn't reality. "I'll be right back, okay?"

I got up and grabbed his clothes from the floor. They were extremely oversized. I slipped them on, anyway. "I'm going downstairs to get a Tylenol," I said before closing the door behind me.

I lied! I grabbed my purse and my phone and headed out. I didn't wanna leave, but I knew I had to. Enough time had been wasted pretending. I called an Uber to the hotel. Uber was the shit… fastest service I've ever seen transportation-wise. Ten minutes later, the car pulled up and I hopped in.

"Long night?" the driver asked, greeting me.

I just gave a nod and sunk down in the back seat. I didn't feel like talking to anyone. I was contemplating what my next move would be when I got there. I had no idea, but I was ready for however this was gonna play out.

After about an hour and a half, I was home, right back where I started. This time would be different, though. I looked around the neighborhood admiring the scenery. It was beautiful. Children playing outside in the snow, couples sitting on the porch watching their babies, nothing was outta place. I looked at my own front door, wanting nothing more than to bust the windows and kick open the doors to air everything out. I needed someone to tell me that my shit was normal and I wasn't the only one living in this fucking fantasy world where people truly valued marriage.

I got out the car and approached the house. I was ready to finally face the music. I walked in and looked around…didn't see Moe . Quietly, I walked around, heart pounding, damn near sweating bullets, yet I needed to look my husband in the eyes and hear the truth. He owed me that. I felt my phone vibrate. Looking down, there was a message from Jasper.

Message read:

"If you let it go, and it comes back~ it's yours. If it doesn't, it never was."

I powered the phone off. I didn't need any distractions once I entered this room. I walked into the kitchen to find Moe sitting on the floor, leaned up against the fridge. Observing Moe, I noticed to the left of him a fifth of Don Julio almost empty and his gun laying on his lap. He stared at me...

He cocked his head to the side, taking a side-eye glimpse of me, then he chuckled to himself.

"Yeah... you must still have amnesia, 'cause I know damn well you ain't got that nigga's clothes on." He took another a sip of his drink.

"You fucked that nigga?"

This was Deja vu! "That's all you ever think about huh-fucking. Not the fact that you've lied this whole time and had me thinking we were good. Not the fact that day-in and day-out you let me think I was fucking going crazy...or the fact that that same bitch who tore our shit apart was just in our garage last week back at this house with you..." He didn't listen to a word I said to him. He grabbed the bottle and downed the remainder of the liquor... Tears streaming down his face, he repeated,

"You gave him some pussy?"

"You didn't love me enough to walk away from her, did you? Look at you... look what you've done to us."

"Ain't like you worried about me. Hell, you coming from

where your concern is."

"You did this!"

"I know how we can solve this," Moe whispered, attempting to get up, but stumbling... catching his balance, but falling back into the fridge, knocking everything on top over to the floor.

He stands up right and looks at me, then down to his gun that's suddenly in his hand.

"My peace can be OUR peace," he said. "I should kill you," he said, pointing the gun at me, "then kill myself," pointing the gun to his chin. He steps forward...

I realized then his peace meant his gun.... killing us both was the remedy.

"I won't have to worry about you with him...and you ain't gotta worry 'bout me with her."

He raised his gun pointing it at me. I couldn't chance this nor call these actions a bluff. This was a side of him I'd never seen and the liquor intensified the situation.

"Don't take another step towards me. I'm not dying for you or anybody else. I've been through enough. If God wanted me to go, I would've been dead... it wasn't my time then and it ain't my time now."

I pulled the gun from Jasper's pocket and I pointed it at Moe.

"Don't take another step, or I'll pull this trigger, got

dammit, I'm not playing."

"You ain't gon' pull shit. I taught you everything you know. Look at you standing there shaking…can't even hold it right. You don't know nothing 'bout no gun!"

With tears streaming down my face, I tried to calm my nerves. My reflexes caused me to wipe the tears and Moe launched at me, knocking the gun from my hand, sending it flying across the floor into the next room.

Moe grabbed me, pulling me close to him with his left arm, his right hand pointing the gun at my head. I stood there with my back to his chest feeling his heart pounding. My eyes were closed. Moe started talking in my ear.

"We gone die together. It's the only answer to this shit. I'm not 'bout to live without you, baby. You're mine 'til death. Didn't I tell you that?" He cocked the gun, ready to pull the trigger.

He'd said his last words to me. I knew I was about to go. I just stood there… Hearing the loud noise from the gun, my body hit the floor.

Damn, that was quick… I didn't feel any pain. Is this what Heaven felt like? I thought I could hear someone calling my name. From the ringing in my ear from the shots, I wasn't sure…but it got closer and closer. I felt something wet and cold on my arms…

OMAR

It seemed my life was in shambles. I felt hopeless. I indulged in bad habits like eating lots of fast food and smoking. I'd picked up an old teenage habit and started back smoking weed. In fact, I was indulging right now. Laying back, having a lil sip of cognac and smoking seemed to ease my mind. This was so unlike me. I was the healthy guy, but life's troubles had taken me under. I stopped at a light pondering over the things I had succumbed to.

"This light is long as hell," I thought to myself. I rolled down my window to begin breaking down my bag, tossing the stems and seeds out the window. I wasn't a pro. In fact, I could hear those friends of mine calling me a lame, but Kush was way too strong for me. All I needed was a little breather, enough to relax my mind... you know...just enough to let my conscious flow.

As the light changed to green, I quickly tried to roll up the window and take off. That's when I thought I saw someone I knew. Was I tripping? Can't be-I haven't even smoked, yet. I sped up in my car, trying to catch up with the car that was on the side of me, hoping they get caught at the next light. Sure enough, they did. As I eased up next to the car, my eyes caught her... De! I didn't know whether to blow the horn or what. My mind said to let her go, but my heart told me to stop her. The driver was some white dingy nerd dude. "Where the heck is she going, and who is she with?"

My last thoughts of being at the hospital wanting to see her crept back into my mind, but I fought them off. I have to talk to her one last time before I go. I followed the car, as she pulled up in front of a house. I wondered if I was making a mistake. Should I just leave? She jumped out the car and stood there looking around.

I watched as her ride drove away. She had on a baggy black Polo jogging suit. The clothes were way too big; it had to be her husband's outfit. I watched as she stood there staring at the house. I attempted to open my door and get out, but I froze in my steps as I watched her pull a gun out her pocket, look down at it, then place it back inside the pocket as she headed for the door. "What is she up to?"

I was so confused, but I couldn't leave here without talking to her. My heart wouldn't let me. I quietly got out my car leaving the door open. As I approached the porch, I could hear commotion and loud voices in the house. The door cracked open allowing me to hear everything. I was at a standstill in the hallway of the front door listening to De and this sorry husband of hers go at it-but this conversation gave me chills. It was dreadful. I worried that I was about to enter something I wouldn't walk away from. I was no punk by far, but I wasn't stupid, either.

One thing my dad taught me as a man was to mind my business. He always said "no need to mind others' business unless it affects you." Well, this here was affecting me, because there I stood in another man's home with my heart tied to his wife. But I loved De. I couldn't help it. I had to know for sure if we were over. I guess I needed closure. I took a few steps forward during every loud shout, trying to drown the sounds of my footsteps with their loud voices. The argument between them was becoming more and more intense. Damn-near suicidal. A wall was the only barrier I had from touching De, but I dared not. I heard her say he had a gun, and I knew she had one, too. I was at a loss for what I could do in this situation.

I went to thinking that maybe I should have hit the blunt before walking into this mess. As I stood there waiting on my next move, the words Moe said shook me. "I'm gonna kill you, then me." Rage ran through my veins and I couldn't contain my anger.

"This weak ass nigga..." I got ready to cut around the wall when a lot of movement took place. I could hear some tussling. Then a gun slid straight across the floor in front of me. Was this meant to be? Based on the conversation, he had knocked the gun De had out of her hand, and there it was laying there at my feet as if Someone was helping me out. Wow! I quickly grabbed the gun off the floor and cut around the wall. I stood there facing the back of this bitch ass nigga's head. He was so drunk, he didn't know I was even there.

I stood there watching him with De in his arms, and a gun to her head. I knew I would never be able to live with myself watching this nigga kill her. I just couldn't! With a swift pull of the trigger I let out one shot. De hit the floor first, and so did I. I shook, thinking I missed him, but the puddle of blood beginning to seep from his head told my otherwise. Naw, I ain't miss him, not at all, but my concern was if I had fulfilled his wishes and shot De as well. My hands and feet went numb and my mouth got dry. "I fucked up!" I shouted! "De... De.... De... Please, God..." I crawled on the floor to her laxed body. "De..." I grabbed her, pulling her to me. I didn't see a gunshot wound anywhere. I just held her in my arms, rocking her. No words needed to be spoken.

DEANNA

I couldn't tell if I was dreaming, dead, or alive. If this was death, it wasn't so bad. I couldn't feel any pain. All I felt was ringing from the gunshot in my ears. I swear the ringing was so strong, it was sounding like it was calling my name. I then felt my body lift off the floor. "Yes, God, I'm ready. Float me to your pearly white gates." I realized after awhile that the voice saying my name was familiar...the scent of his cologne sparked a flame. The gentle hands that rubbed my back and rocked me had touched me before. Omar... As he rocked me back and forth, silence fell over the room. All I could hear was a vibration.

My chin lay on Omar's shoulder as I looked at my cell phone lying next to Moe's dead body. It was Jasper. I stared at the phone, watching his number flash across my screen. I knew I would never be with Jasper again. My fate had been chosen by Omar. Replaying the last moments in my head, I stared at the cabinet where a bullet was launched where I stood pressed against Moe. I had no emotions for what just occurred. I couldn't believe he was actually gon' kill me. I no longer had a fuck to give, nor a tear to shed. Moe and I both could have been lying there on the floor dead... Once again, I had cheated death.

FOLLOW ME @...

Facebook:
@Author Casey Carter

Instagram:
@ccthenursewriter

Twitter:
@Casey_Dann

Website:
blaccberryfantasies.com

E-mail:
authorcaseycarter@gmail.com

CPSIA information can be obtained
at www.ICGtesting.com
Printed in the USA
LVOW13s1522270417

532420LV00008B/654/P